Get Your
Coventry Romances
Home Subscription NOW

And Get These
4 Best-Selling Novels
FREE:

LACEY
by Claudette Williams

THE ROMANTIC WIDOW
by Mollie Chappell

HELENE
by Leonora Blythe

THE HEARTBREAK TRIANGLE
by Nora Hampton

A Home Subscription! It's the easiest and most convenient way to get every one of the exciting Coventry Romance Novels! . . .And you get 4 of them FREE!

You pay nothing extra for this convenience: there are no additional charges. . .you don't even pay for postage! Fill out and send us the handy coupon now, and we'll send you 4 exciting Coventry Romance novels absolutely FREE!

SEND NO MONEY, GET THESE
FOUR BOOKS
FREE!

Joan Smith

REPRISE

FAWCETT COVENTRY • NEW YORK

REPRISE

Published by Fawcett Coventry Books, CBS Educational and Professional Publishing, a division of CBS Inc.

ISBN: 0-449-50284-8

Printed in the United States of America

First Fawcett Coventry printing: April 1982

10 9 8 7 6 5 4 3 2 1

1

"*Well, my pets,* so you are still house hunting," Lady Melvine said. "You must be fagged to death with it. There is nothing so wearing. You know you are always welcome to stay with me, but I see by your little smiles, Dammler, you hope to have your bride to yourself for the treacle moon." She glanced at her nephew and his fiancée, marveling anew at the odd match. Dammler, an eminently eligible marquess, a poet and the most handsome rogue in London. What did he see in this little spinster that he should smile on her so fondly?

"I'm gypping Prue out of the treacle moon, Het. I don't think it's wise to do her out of a house of her own as well. We must stay in town for part of the summer to see to my play, you know."

"Ah yes, *Shilla* will be opening in September, will it not, your new play? You have rehearsals to attend, I suppose."

"Also some rewriting, costumes and so on."

"And three dozen black wigs for all those harem girls," Hettie added. His play involved his oriental travels that had had their first airing in *Cantos from Abroad,* a book of his poetry that had catapulted him to fame a year before.

"The cast is dyed," he told her, then hunched his elegant shoulders in a disparaging way that set her looking for a little joke in his words.

"Ah yes, I see it now," she said a moment later. "And soon the die will be cast as well, with your wedding. It seems to me you chose a devilish busy time for it."

"We didn't want to wait," he told her. The eagerness, strangely enough, appeared to be all on his side. But then Prudence Mallow was a perfect oyster. She had to be well pleased with her catch, and anxious to get him to the altar.

"Our choices of house seem to be limited to two," Prudence outlined. "We can take Devonshire House with twenty-four bedrooms at a ruinous cost, or an apartment in what Allan calls limbo, meaning Upper Grosvenor Square, with twenty-four square inches. You'd think with the season over and everyone leaving town, houses would be going begging."

"We are thinking of throwing up a tent in Green Park," Dammler said, smiling ruefully.

"We could get fresh milk from the herd of cattle, too," Prudence added.

"I would like it excessively," Dammler took it up. He was always eager to talk any nonsense. "I am pretty good at throwing up a tent from my travels, and could teach you to milk a cow in jig time."

"As you already know how to milk the cow, there is no need to teach *me*," she pointed out. "You forget we are a busy working couple. You aren't the only one who can read and write. I don't plan to cosset you, you know."

"You see how she treats me," Dammler complained to Hettie, with still that provoking smile on his face. He saw not a fault in his beloved. That she occasionally dashed off a novel set her quite up in her own conceit, Hettie thought. "She'll have me fetching and carrying and acting as footman to tote her volumes to Murray, our publisher."

"You want to trim her into line before you put the ring on her finger," Hettie laughed, sliding in a piece of advice under the guise of a joke.

"I mean to get her well under my legal control before I straighten her out," he replied. "Then the story will change. I have not been unaffected by my little trip around the world. I have taken copious notes on how these matters are managed in the east."

"I expect you refer to harems and such things. You will pray confine your seraglio to the stage, Allan," Prudence told him with a pert smile.

"Yes, Mama," he said obediently, but with a gleaming eye, "if you *really want* me to carry on my amorous intrigues in the full glare of the public eye."

She shook her head at him with a weary sigh. He was quite simply incorrigible. She doubted she could quite control this reformed rake. How she had ever wrested him away from his mistress, Cybele, was still a mystery to her. She was a gorgeous thing, but still he had abandoned her and come running after herself to Bath when she had fled him after a quarrel. "What would you do if you were stuck with such a husband, Lady Melvine?" she asked, smiling.

"I would buy him a chastity belt and hide the key," Hettie answered promptly, then walked off laughing. Maybe it would work out. Prudence was not beautiful and she was not rich, but she seemed to have something that appealed to Allan, some way of handling him that the more attractive girls did not, and really he would require careful handling.

"What on earth is a chastity belt?" Prudence asked her laughing lover.

"You'll find out, the first time I have to leave you after we are married," he told her.

"If it serves the function its name suggests, it is you who will require one. No, not one, a dozen."

"I have one that is as good as a hundred. You." He touched the tip of her nose and folded her arm posses-

7

sively under his to resume their walk. "Whenever I am tempted . . . No, I am never tempted. I am cured of all that sort of thing. How would you like to live on a houseboat, Prue? We might buy a fancy yacht and set up house on the Thames."

"Excellent! At midnight I would pull up the gangplank and catch you out every time you tried to sneak home late."

"Then nail it up on the other side and make me walk it, right into the drink, if my breath smelled of liquor."

"How managing you make me sound! I don't plan to measure the level of the decanters. I shall seal them up with wax instead," she added, with an arch smile.

"We'll be too busy working to fall into dissipation. You have your novel to finish and I my play. The devil finds work for idle hands. He's the busiest employer there ever was. Ah, speak of the devil. Here is Uncle Clarence."

Glancing up, Prudence saw her uncle heave into view. A dapper little gentleman of middle years outfitted in the highest kick of fashion, he was a prime favorite with Dammler, who always suffered a fool gladly.

"Not at your easel this afternoon, Uncle?" he asked. Uncle Clarence called himself an artist. He used up more canvas and pigment than all of the real artists of London put together, dashing off a likeness of anyone with nothing better to do for three afternoons than sit for him. Three afternoons was the time required for him to splash up a masterpiece.

"Giving the old eyes a rest," Clarence assured them. "Have you found a place to squat after the wedding?"

"We were just discussing the possibilities of Green Park," Prudence mentioned.

"Aye, that would be nothing new for you, eh, Nevvie?

You must have spent many a night under canvas in Africa or America. They would have no houses in America. I can't think why you went there and got yourself all shot up." He just glanced to Dammler's eyebrow, where a slight irregularity at one end was all that remained of a shot from an arrow.

"It wouldn't be the first time for me," Dammler agreed, "but this comfort-craving wife of mine wouldn't care for sleeping on the ground."

"Comfort crazy! You have hit it on the head," Clarence told him. "She has got a new chair for her study—a stuffed chair, very fine it is. Blue velvet. Cost me—well, you wouldn't be interested to hear the sum I paid for it. Daresay it would seem little enough to you; still, ten guineas is a high price for a chair, even an upholstered chair."

"You spoil her, Uncle. How am I expected to keep pace with such a high style as you set?" Dammler asked, his eyes twinkling.

Clarence was well pleased with his own comfortable but plain abode, and perceived no humor in this. "You are welcome to come along and be spoiled with her. As for me, I must ankle along home. Your aunt is having us to her little rout party this evening, and I really ought to get in an hour at my easel."

"Don't let us keep you, Uncle," Prudence said at once. "We are off to visit a friend of a half-cousin's wife who *might* know a lady with a house to let."

"Excellent! There is nothing like close friends when all's said and done. I wish you well. I'll nip along to the corner where I am to meet my phaeton. My new high perch phaeton." He bowed and walked jauntily on, summoning all his courage and physical reserve for the dangerous vault into his high perch phaeton. Since coming into a nephew from the very apex of society,

9

Clarence Elmtree was busy to ape all the more *outré* modes of the aristocracy.

"Who is he Rembrandting today?" Dammler asked his fiancée.

"Himself. It is all to be laid in your dish, so don't bother laughing at him. Since you gave him that book he has cleared his palette of all his lovely blues and greens and uses nothing but brown and pink. He is after me to stand at the backhouse door with a broom in my hand and my hair falling about my ears, but as I am much too grand for such pastimes these days, he paints himself, like Rembrandt. You have revolutionized his whole technique. No longer does he paint out the warts and moles, but puts them in where nature neglected to do so."

"It was my innocent mention that it took a real artist to make ugliness beautiful that turned him around."

"Hmmm, but I think the ease of filling three-quarters of the canvas with a nice mud-brown helped. He could reduce the sittings to one day if he really wanted to, but has become accustomed to three." She smiled fondly at her uncle's folly.

Clarence had used to paint nothing but daVincis, but since discovering the ease of a brown canvas with a round pink face highlighted in the center, he was busy making Rembrandt famous. "The fellow can paint no more than a good face, but he does the faces dashed well," he had confided to them. "The hands, now, he has as good as eliminated, and by sticking the subject in a doorway or window he does away with proportion and foreshortening and all the rest of it." For any unartistic critic who voiced a complaint of this technique, he had his setdown ready. "Chiaroscuro," he would announce grandly, and go on to utter some mention of light and shade in a way to show the *artist* knew what he was about, even if the critic didn't. Subjects were less eager to be done in this unbecoming guise than as Mona Lisa, so that Uncle had often to doff his new jacket by Stultz and don his brown dressing gown to pose for himself. He disliked having such a dull audience, and was more apt to be seen dashing along Bond Street in his new phaeton, or calling on some of the mighty who were soon to be connected to him. He had made a firm friend of Hettie, who adored eccentrics.

"Prue, about this house business," Dammler said, interrupting her reverie. "What do you say to buying one? There are plenty for sale, and so few for rent. We'll be needing one permanently. We'll want to spend some part of the season at least in town each year, and with our writing will often have to come in from Longbourne Abbey. It's a good investment, too. Trevor Place on Berkeley Square is going at a good price. Shall we go have a look at it?"

"It's getting quite late. Why don't I hail Uncle Clarence on his way past and you go on and look at it? If you like it, I'll go back with you tomorrow."

"All right. I see Uncle is coming this way now. I'll hail him down. You'll have to look nimble to clamber in at one leap as Clarence does." He stopped the carriage and turned back to Prudence. "Eight-thirty tonight?"

"Yes."

Dammler stood on the corner, watching them leave. When Prudence turned to have a last look at him, he blew her a kiss, and felt like running after the carriage and going with her. He didn't like to be away from her for a moment. He had wanted to be married in Bath three weeks earlier when they had patched up their differences and become engaged. The romance had flowered from an unlikely professional friendship instigated by John Murray, their publisher. Prudence was a country girl with modest ideas and a brain and pen Dammler envied. He had admired first her splendid novels, then her mind, and only last her body. The polite world thought Miss Mallow had done very well for herself to nab Lord Dammler, but Allan knew he was the fortunate one. He had been bent on a road to self-destruction when he had met Prue. His much-admired poetry he considered melodramatic stuff, flashy wordplay that caught the eye but would not endure ten years. His real interest had been in amusement and women, horses, partying. Now all that was changed. His play to open in October was better than his poetry because he had fashioned his heroine, *Shilla,* after Prudence.

For once, what was right and good coincided exactly with what he wanted—a good useful life with Prue. He intended settling down to some serious writing and serious reforming. He had got rid of all his flirts and of course his mistress, Cybele. He had ceased to find amusement in any of them after meeting Prudence. She had been appalled at his way of carrying on, though she had tried to hide it, but he meant to show her all that was behind him. Unfortunate that he had inadvertently drawn her a little into his own raffish set, making her known to people that were too fast for her. There had been in particular a Mr. Seville, the memory of whom still caused Dammler's hands to clench into fists. A man-about-town with an unsavory reputation, he had taken to dangling after her, and though he had ultimately offered to marry her, Dammler could never quite believe the fellow was serious. He had said some things to Hettie that did not ring true—some little insinuation that what he had offered was not a gold ring but a carte blanche. But all that was in

12

the past. In two weeks they would be married, and go to Longbourne Abbey for a short honeymoon before returning to London for the play. In his mind he saw himself seated at a desk in a quiet corner of a study, with Prudence across from him writing on her latest novel, *Patience*. A quiet, useful life.

He shook the thought from his head reluctantly and grabbed a passing hackney cab to go to Berkeley Square to view the house for sale. It was the right size, the right address, and the right price. Needed work, but it was worth bringing Prudence to have a look at it.

He was so weary of looking that he was resolved to have the place unless she took it in violent dislike. But she never disliked anything he liked, or if she did, she was too nice to say so. She was enthusiastic about the house even before she saw it the next morning, and was vastly impressed with the splendor of twelve faded bedrooms, when he was a little afraid it was too few.

"The saloon wouldn't hold above fifty comfortably," he pointed out apologetically.

"Fifty! I'm sure we'd never be entertaining *fifty* people at once," she answered. Twelve was a largish party at Elmtree's home. It was on such occasions as these that Prudence felt a little trepidation regarding her future. Their pasts were really so very different that there would be a good deal of adjusting to be done, and she foresaw the majority of it would be done by herself.

"For balls you know—but we can hold them *chez* Hettie. She will adore it. The study is nice and spacious— room for two desks, and not too far apart either, just as I like."

"My two shelves of books will fit nicely right *here*," she pointed out, making a joking reference to her paucity of books. "And you can put your ten thousand on the other side," she added.

13

"Shall we put an offer on it then? I'm dog-tired with looking, and the wedding's only two weeks away. *Only!* That's fourteen days too long to suit me."

She nodded her agreement. "Your days are numbered, Dammler. Enjoy your freedom while you can, for in two weeks you will be leashed, and have to account to me for your time."

"I do already—haven't you noticed? Tonight I have a bachelor's dinner at the Reddleston—some of my friends from Cambridge. I sha'n't stop in later, for the thing will go on till dawn. I'll put a down payment on the house this afternoon, which will involve long and very dull sessions with my banker—if you're sure you're satisfied? The furniture goes with it. Half of it useless lumber, but at least we'll have a table and chairs. And a bed—an item of considerable importance to the more libidinous among us. We can replace the rest by degrees."

"Fine—I like it very much. It's good to have it settled. And you mustn't worry that the owner stripped the walls of paintings. Uncle will splatter us up a bunch of Mona Lisas or Rembrandts—whatever you fancy."

"I'll see you tomorrow then, and we'll come back here and go over the place to see what you want done to it to make it habitable immediately. I'll drop by Hettie's place this afternoon. She'll be dying to hear we're settled *at last*. She'll want to come around and see it for herself, but I'll close the deal before she begins discovering watermarks on the ceiling and cracked walls. Personally, I don't care if the ceilings are black and blue, as long as the roof stands over our heads."

"You have to see Wills about your play this afternoon, too."

"Not a minute for me to fall into the devil's clutches, you see. From banker to Wills. Come, I'll take you

14

home. I don't mean to let you walk the streets alone, my girl. Satan may have an eye on you, too, now that you've fallen into my orbit."

They went happily off to Grosvenor Square discussing the future, without a single thought that Satan was lurking around the corner, planning the greatest mischief for them.

2

Lady Melvine was not only Dammler's aunt, but his best friend in London outside of Prudence Mallow. He told her of his new house that afternoon, and she was eager to see it, but his visit with Wills made it impossible. The next morning she was up bright and early, had her carriage taken round to Grosvenor Square, and installed herself in Clarence's saloon to await the trip to Berkeley Square.

When Clarence heard who sat in his saloon, he was soon pushing away his eggs half-eaten and dashing to see her. Prudence smiled across the table to her mother. "Good—this will give us a chance to finish our meal in peace. Hettie means to go and see the house, I suppose. Will you come with us too, Mama?"

"I'll go another time, dear. Four in the carriage will be enough."

"We are only three. Oh, Uncle Clarence! Of course he will want to come along."

"It would be a nice gesture to ask him," her mother replied.

Mrs. Mallow's brother Clarence had for several years provided the two ladies a roof over their heads free of cost, and his wishes were always deferred to in these little matters.

"Certainly I'll ask him," Prudence said happily. It was one of life's little mysteries to her that Clarence rubbed along so well with all Dammler's relatives. Truth to tell, she had been half ashamed to produce him for inspection, but from the first he had made a hit. It was his lack of any sense of inferiority in himself that put him over. He was as undaunted by public opinion as those exalted personages who considered themselves well above public censure. He *cared* for approval, but never once was bothered by the idea that he might not attain it.

Her breakfast finished, Prudence went to the saloon to find Clarence already dressed for the street, with his hat in his hand, his gloves on and malacca walking stick at the ready.

"Good morning, Lady Melvine. Are you coming with us to Berkeley Square?" she asked.

"Indeed I am. What time is Dammler calling for you?"

"No hour was set actually. He expected to be up late after the bachelor party."

"He said *early!*" Hettie advised her.

"We'll go and wake him up," Clarence said at once, very eager to be into Lady Melvine's carriage. More eager for this treat than to see the house, actually.

"I wouldn't like to do that, Uncle," Prudence said, hoping to restrain him.

"*I'll* take the responsibility," Hettie said. "He told me early, the wretch, and I had myself called at the ungodly hour of eight-thirty on purpose."

Clarence, who never arose later than eight, said "Eight-thirty! You are an early riser!"

"Not usually, but as the villain got me up at the crack of dawn, I'll haul him out by the ear. See if I don't."

After a few more attempts at stalling, Prudence was talked into going by the others, and they all three set off to Dammler's rooms at Albany. When the carriage pulled up to the door, Clarence alit to open the door for the ladies, but said he would "just wait outside," for he

17

had high hopes that some friend would chance by and see him lounging at his ease inside a crested carriage, and he would be able to tell him he awaited his nevvie, Lord Dammler, the poet.

Prudence and Hettie went inside, their eyes accustomed from a few visits to the eastern decor of the place. Ottomans and leather hassocks stood in lieu of sofas and chairs. The tables, too, were brought back from Persia, short tables with nacre inlays, and one trivet table made entirely of brass. It was odd and interesting rather than beautiful. "The brothel," Hettie called it quite bluntly.

The butler appeared not only surprised but acutely uncomfortable to see them in, and asked them to await his lordship in the saloon. They accepted this, but had not been seated a minute till Hettie arose saying, "I'll go and hurry him along. He's probably sound asleep." Prudence nodded and remained where she was, but after a few minutes she decided to continue her wait in Dammler's library, always a place of interest to her.

The library took her next door to Dammler's bedroom, and as the door stood partially open, she could hear very distinctly what was being said.

"How did you come to *do* such a thing!" Hettie exclaimed, in a very shocked voice, and she was not a lady who was easily shocked.

"It just happened. I can't explain now. For God's sake get rid of her, Hettie. Get Prudence out of here."

"What excuse can I use?"

"Say I'm sick—say what you like, but get her out of here!"

Prudence stood listening, thinking she must have misheard, misunderstood. Dammler was *furious* that she had come. Why should he be?

He spoke again. "I'll meet you at Berkeley Square in

18

half an hour. Now *go,* before she comes in and catches me like this." His voice sounded deranged.

She didn't know what to think. Within the space of seconds she envisaged him ill, wounded, suffering from some disfiguring disease or accident. She took a step towards the door, her heart in her mouth, prepared, she thought, for anything. She found she was mistaken. She certainly was not prepared to see him standing hale and hearty in a flamboyant dressing gown with a cup of coffee in his hand and a voluptuous blond lady in his bed, with a table set for two beside it. The female wore next to nothing—some scanty bit of white diaphanous material, possibly an undergarment.

Prudence took one step into the room and two back. Then she advanced again, slowly, looking around at the disorder of the chamber—an evening gown thrown over a table, silk stockings on the floor, Dammler's coat hanging on a door knob. Then she looked at the female. She was exquisite. A cloud of platinum curls, a pair of large green eyes, a heart-shaped face. The girl opened red lips and laughed inanely, revealing perfect teeth. "Who are you?" she asked in a sweet, childish voice.

Prudence didn't answer the question, nor was it necessary for her to return it. She knew well enough who this vision was. Cybele. Dammler's former mistress, still current mistress, as well. She had seen them together before at the opera. Cybele was not the sort of apparition one could forget, hard as she might try. Prudence stood a long minute staring at her, longer than she wanted to. While she kept her eyes riveted on Cybele, she didn't have to look at Dammler. She couldn't bear to look at him, but as though her eyes had a will of their own, they turned to him, pulling her head with them. He looked awful—sick and frightened, the way she felt. Her lips moved but no words came out.

19

"Prudence," he said. It was hardly even a whisper—just a low sigh of regret.

"Why?" she asked him, the one word all she could utter.

He couldn't manage an answer. He just stood, looking at her, as guilty as sin. Then he closed his eyes and squeezed them shut hard, as though to block out his vision of her. When he opened them half a minute later, she was gone. With the last vestige of her strength and wits, she had turned and fled the room, fled the apartment and the building. Clarence was still in the carriage. She got in and said, "Take me home."

He thought she was ill; she looked so white, her eyes moist and staring. He shouted to Lady Melvine's groom to "Spring 'em." He would have liked to ask her questions, but deemed her too sick to answer. The novelty of this rather pleased him. Dammler would be dashing over in a minute to see how she did. He would send for Knighton, the royal family's and his own physician. A little notice in the *Observer*, perhaps, would not go amiss.

Back at the apartment, Hettie took Dammler in hand. "Go after her. Make up some story," she advised him.

"Hettie, I don't have to *lie!* It's not what you think."

"My dear, it is not in the least necessary to sham it with me. I recognize your ladybird." She smiled quite cordially at Cybele, who smiled back, then hopped out of bed, revealing her gorgeous body, only nominally covered by the wisp of chiffon.

"Get back in there!" Dammler shouted. She pouted, but obeyed him on the instant.

Hettie fairly swooned with delight. She hadn't had such fun in months, and it cheered her to discover Miss Mallow didn't have such a tight line on Dammler as

20

she had thought. Really it was a shame for him to go getting married so soon. While these thoughts flitted through her mind, Dammler was pulling off his dressing gown, tossing it to the floor, grabbing up a jacket, all in a state of terrible distraction.

"Stay here!" he called to Cybele, then flew out the door with his black hair falling across his forehead. The carriage was gone. He rushed into the street, hailing a passing cab. He hopped in and directed it to Clarence Elmtree's address, assuming Prudence had gone home, as indeed she had, arriving there five minutes before him. She hadn't said a word to Clarence, who thus ushered Nevvie straight into his best saloon, where she had succumbed to shock on the sofa.

"Nevvie is come to see how you go on. I have sent a boy off for Knighton. He will have her up and about in no time," he said aside to Dammler. "A very sudden fit came over her. Gave me quite a turn. A weakness—I suppose it is nerves. She was always nervous," he rambled on. Then as the two remained rigid, glaring at each other like gladiators about to enter combat, he decided to leave them to it. A little lovers' tiff. They would patch it up better without an audience.

Dammler was the first to speak. "I can explain everything, Prudence."

"I'm not a moron. When I see your mistress in your bed, I know what to think."

"I was drunk," he said, a desperate note creeping into his voice. "You know I had a bachelor's party thrown for me last night. It's part of the ritual to try to drink the groom under the table."

"Is it part of the ritual to drink him under the sheets, too?" she asked.

"There were no *girls* there, if that's what you're implying."

21

"Where was Cybele? At home waiting for you?"

"No! Well—yes, in a way she was. She came to the apartment while I was out, and my butler let her in. She had run away from her latest patron. He was drunk as a skunk and threatened to beat her. She didn't know where to go, poor girl, and ran back to me."

"She knew where to go, all right! She knew where she'd be welcome." She suddenly noticed her voice was high, strident. She hadn't thought she'd be able to say a word, but found she was glad to vent her anger on him. How *dare* he ruin her life?

"She wasn't welcome! Drunk as I was, I knew she shouldn't stay."

"But she *did* stay, didn't she, Dammler? She stayed and spent the night with you!"

"Yes, she stayed. What was I supposed to do—turn her out in the streets at three o'clock in the morning? Have a heart, Prudence."

"I have a heart, and I have eyes and a mind too, and my mind doesn't like what my eyes see. How could you *do* such a thing? Our wedding only two weeks away!"

"I don't know. At three o'clock this morning, it seemed the right, the charitable thing to do, and to hell with convention."

"You were never much of a one for convention, but you've outdone even yourself this time. I didn't like the fact that you *had* a mistress before our engagement. I didn't like your constantly dashing off to Finefields with Lady Malvern, and quite frankly, I didn't like many of the things you said to me, an unmarried lady. Too unconventional for my simple tastes. I was right. I should have listened to myself. You're too far beyond convention for me."

"You're not going to break off our marriage just because I let Cybele stay overnight!" he shouted, in the tone of a command, but the anger in his voice was edged with fear. Already he was regretting not having pushed the wedding ahead in Bath.

"The very fact that you think it negligible makes me realize how different we are. I think it was a *gross, unforgivable, horrible* thing for you to do. I couldn't believe my eyes when I saw it. I was . . ." She stopped, unable to find words to express her disgust.

"I know you were," he said, apparently reading her mind. "Prudence, I'd do anything if this could have been prevented."

"It *could* have been, Allan! It was surely not impossible for you to put her into your carriage and send her to an hotel, or go to one yourself."

"I didn't think of that! I wish I had. I told you I'd been drinking. I meant to send her away this morning."

"And never tell me a word about it. I'm glad I went. I'm glad I saw you two together. It may be horrible for a while, but I'll get over it. We would never have suited. I'm not marrying you."

She pulled the engagement ring from her finger and handed it to him.

"You don't trust me. That's what you're saying," he said, reproachful, but still angry.

"Yes, that is exactly what I am saying. I no more trust you with Cybele than I'd trust a dog with a roast."

"I didn't sleep with her."

"I think you did."

"I tell you I didn't!" he shouted, the pulse in his temple throbbing. He looked at her, waiting, but he saw no signs of wavering, of backing down. "Well?"

"That's your story, and you're welcome to stick to it. In that case I expect *I* shall be indicted as the villain of the piece, turning you off for no good reason. A flirt—a jilt! A new role for me. As well some of the bloom has

23

been brushed off my innocence by association with you. Three months ago no one would have believed it of me, but a lady who managed to get herself engaged to *you* will be considered up to anything. *Your* gilded reputation will escape untarnished—this time."

"You know I don't give a damn about that."

"You don't give a damn about anything except chasing girls. Go on—go back to her. Give her the diamond ring. You had her dripping with gems from ears to wrists, but you neglected to give her a diamond ring you once told me."

His nostrils flared dangerously. She expected some searing tirade, but he just turned and strode out of the room. She sat on alone with dry eyes, her shoulders sagging, listening as he banged his way down the hall, out the front door. Then she went up to her room and cried on the bed.

3

Clarence had a busy day. He realized there was some little altercation between the lovebirds, but was too much the optimist to consider it serious. Prudence's mother, Wilma, shook her head sadly and told him he'd better send in the notice to the papers canceling the wedding, but he pooh-poohed this as nonsense. "A lovers' quarrel. The course of true love never runs smooth. My wife and I had a dozen fallings out. You don't go turning off a marquess just for that."

"It is more serious than that, Clarence. The fact is, he had a *woman* in his apartment."

"What of that? He's a poet. Some lady or other calling on him. They are a trifle unconventional."

"It wasn't a *lady*," she said discreetly, hoping she would have to say no more.

"By gad . . . You mean . . ." He cocked an eyebrow and gave a sly little smile. She nodded her head.

"The rascal! He is up to all the rigs. And the wedding not two weeks off. I should think he could have waited . . . Well, well. So that is why she is in the boughs! I thought it was something serious."

"It *is* serious," Wilma pointed out gently. "I always felt his character to be unsteady. He is a jolly fellow, very easy to like, but I confess I was always worried by his reputation."

"Pooh! What is one more woman to the likes of Dammler? They are all running after him. Prudence is lucky to have a look-in at all. She knew he wasn't a saint."

Wilma rolled an uncomprehending eye at him, and was glad when the door knocker sounded to interrupt them. Not so glad when Dr. Knighton was admitted, and she had the unwelcome chore of telling the foremost physician in London her daughter did not wish to see him.

"I hurried away from Princess Marie to come here!" Knighton said, astonished at such a reception.

Clarence smiled benignly, storing up this lovely morsel for relaying to his crones. "Run back to her," he advised the doctor. "It doesn't do to offend the royal family. They might take it amiss and hire another doctor. Just leave a few drops of something for my niece."

"Your note said it was urgent—*most urgent!*"

"It is. She's too sick to see you," Clarence explained happily. Knighton looked to Mrs. Mallow for guidance, rather wondering whether it wasn't the gentleman before him who was ill of a brain fever.

He was finally gotten rid of, and made a silent vow that he would come no more to Grosvenor Square. Prudence stayed in her room, not melodramatically barring the door and refusing food and drink, but trying manfully to sip and nibble a little something. Her mother spent some time with her, giving her what she felt in her heart was good advice, though it was not the advice the daughter wished to hear. Mrs. Mallow had always had reservations regarding Dammler. Certainly he was handsome, rich, talented, titled, personable and all the rest, but he was too high a flyer for her little Prudence. He was known in several countries as a famous flirt. What had good, simple people like themselves to do with such a man?

"Better you find out what he's like now than later," she consoled. "It will be hard at first, but there was

26

that nice Mr. Springer at Bath who liked you, Prue, and Mr. Seville—you remember he wanted to marry you a month ago—so very eligible."

But Mr. Seville was already married to another, and Mr. Springer only a country gentleman with none of Dammler's charm. There was only one Dammler in the world. She had won him, and she had lost him—to the muslin company. It was for the best, as Mama said, but why must the best seem so dreadfully like the very worst thing imaginable? She couldn't bear to think of life without him. The happy dream of going to Longbourne Abbey, of helping him set up his hostel for unmarried mothers, of working and writing side-by-side with him both there and in London, of being included in the opening of his play, *Shilla and the Mogul*—all of it. Every single act of her future life had held the promise of bliss, and now it was reduced to this nothingness. To continue living with Uncle Clarence and Mama, doing the same dull things she had been doing forever, seeing Dammler no more. Or worse—could it possibly be worse?—seeing him with someone else, some other girl, and eventually a wife.

It was her own fault. She should never have allowed herself to fall in love with such a man, a notorious womanizer, really. His first fame was based on a public disclosure of his international affairs. Disguised of course, but based on fact. She knew all that, and idiot that she was, had thought she could reform him. Thought she *had* reformed him. He was not capable of reform, and this proved it. The thing to do was to put him out of her mind, forget she had ever known him. She had not been miserable before knowing him. She had been content, even happy when Murray had taken a couple of books. She would be happy again. Her eyes fell on her wedding gown, a beautiful white crêpe de chine, an

27

extravagant thing that Allan had insisted on, and paid for, incidentally. More lack of convention. More weakness on her part, to have let him. She had let him change her too much, too easily. Broad-minded they called it, to smile at their friends' lovers and affairs, but before knowing him she would have called it sinful, and so it was. This was what came of it. Now she was expected to be broad-minded about her groom, but she hadn't changed that much, and she thanked God for it.

It was a combination of anger and religion that overcame her weakness, her deep-down desire to take him back, pretend it was all right. It was all wrong, and she wouldn't accept it. What hellish kind of a marriage would it be, with a groom whose hobby was philandering? It would be even worse than this hell. She dried her tears, hardened her heart, and tried to begin formulating some plans. Her work—at least she had that. Her latest novel, *Patience*, had lain half finished for weeks. She would get back to work at it. Mid-July, with so many people out of town, was a good time for it. By the fall, maybe the worst of it would be over.

Dammler returned to his apartment crestfallen, to find Cybele and Hettie chatting gaily over a cup of cocoa. "How did it go?" his aunt asked him.

."How do you think? She turned me off."

"Ninny. I'll go talk to her."

"I think not, Hettie. But if you want to be of help to me, let us decide what is to be done with Cybele. She can't go back to Danfers. What can we do with her?"

Cybele sat smiling, perfectly satisfied to have her fate arranged in this arbitrary fashion.

"She could go back home to Manchester," Dammler mentioned, over her head.

"I don't like Manchester," she said.

"She'd die of boredom," Hettie said. "And with such a ravishingly pretty creature, there is no point thinking to turn her into a servant or modiste, Allan. She will certainly end up under some gentleman's protection. The thing to do is find a nice gent for her. Vissington is between *chères amies*."

"That old man! Good God, Het. We can do better than that for her. What would you like to do, Cybele?"

"I want to be an actress," she told him, her green eyes star-struck and a smile on her lips. "Can I be in your play?"

"It's a bit late for that. They're well into rehearsals already."

"A small part, Dammler," Hettie took it up. "You could do it for her. It will get her out of your hair, and Wills will arrange accommodation with one of the other actresses. It will do for the present." It was unnecessary to state this vision of loveliness would not long be employed. Some wealthy man would soon have her under his wing.

"Very well. Come along, Cybele," he said.

She got up, obedient as a child, and went with him. Wills accepted her with equanimity. He had two dozen such voluptuous stage props. Dammler's ex-mistress would add a note of interest. He observed, of course, that the woman never spoke above a whisper, which made it impossible to give her any spoken lines, and the hair would be a bit of a problem as Dammler supported the girl in not wanting to have it dyed, but a black wig could be arranged easily enough, and soon it was all arranged, even to quarters shared with another actress who lived above a milliner's shop on Conduit Street at the corner of Bond.

"Thank you," Cybele whispered with a smile. Wills

29

gazed at her, besot, as all men were at her incredible, staggering beauty.

Dammler left and went home to consider his plight. He couldn't believe Prudence had turned him off forever only for this accident. She'd come around in time, but he hoped it wouldn't take too much time, with the wedding only thirteen days away now. He went to his man of business, to his bank, finalizing papers on the new house. Then he went to the house itself, wishing he had got a better one, that it would offer more temptation to Prudence. But he knew really that she would be unswayed by material things. He spent a mixed up day, not able to settle down to either work or sport or socializing. In the evening he remembered he was supposed to take Prudence to a small party at the home of some friends who were still in town. Certainly that must be settled; it made a sufficient excuse to go to her again.

They were to be there at nine. At eight-thirty he was pounding at Clarence's knocker, and was told she was indisposed.

"Knighton has been to see her. He left some drops and she is out like a lamp. You must make her excuses, Nevvie. Drop around in the morning; she will want to see you."

"Did she say so?" he asked, knowing from past experience the futility of asking Clarence a question. He lived in a world of his own, untroubled by reality except as it impinged occasionally on granting him glory.

"Certainly she did," he was assured, and like the party, it was an excuse to return.

He sent in a written excuse for himself and Prudence to the party, then went home, telling himself he was working, when in fact he did no more than pace the

30

apartment, rehearsing things to say to her at their next meeting. Occasionally he took up a book, only to set it aside after two minutes' inattentive perusal. He went early to bed, knowing sleep would not favor him that night. He had the idea of reading one of Prudence's books. It made him feel close to her. He read his favorite, *The Composition*. In it she had turned her painting uncle into a piano-playing aunt. Dammler read it with admiration and amusement. He convinced himself a woman with such wit, discernment and humor would come to her senses and laugh at her own foolish behavior before morning. He'd go back and all would be well again between them.

His opinion was unchanged in the morning, but not so firm that he neglected to scan the notices in all the newspapers. She hadn't sent in any cancellation of the wedding, so she didn't really mean to jilt him. This gave him confidence, but when he got to the front door, doubts began to assail him. He had waited till ten-thirty to come, but still Clarence told him she was in bed. Prudence never slept past eight.

"Step in and sit down. She'll come in a flash when she hears you're here," Clarence told him.

The servant brought word quite simply that Miss Mallow did not wish to see Lord Dammler. "I'll wait," he said, pretending to misunderstand the reply.

"I'll hustle her along," Clarence told him, but when she told him she was through with Dammler for good, he suddenly didn't feel like facing Nevvie again that morning, and went to his studio to paint. He had no model on hand, so painted in the brown edges and did another picture of himself, wearing his nightcap. This solved very nicely the habit his own brown hair had of disappearing into the brown background. It was chiaroscuro of the best sort in his eyes, a nice sharp contrast of white and brown. Dandy. Rembrandt didn't manage it quite so well. Had a way of blurring it all together.

For forty-five minutes Dammler sat alone in the saloon, getting more worried and more angry as he sat. He went into the hall and asked the butler if he might please see *Mrs.* Mallow. She came, disturbed, embarrassed, but firm in her declaration that Prudence would not see him.

"By God she will, if I have to rip down her door," he said. "Would you please tell her so, ma'am."

The message was relayed. "Maybe you'd better just *see* him," Mrs. Mallow suggested.

"I wouldn't see him if my life depended on it. The *impertinence* of giving such a message to you, my mother! Upon my word, he has been unconventional in the past, but this is the first time I have seen an outright display of bad breeding. Tell him to go away, and not come back."

Poor Mrs. Mallow returned below with this unhappy news. She was glad Prudence was firm in her resolve, but when she saw the lost look that came over Dammler's face, she had second thoughts. Even as she stood watching, wavering in her own resolve, she saw a change come over his expression. The hurt look gave way to anger, and soon to resolution.

"Thank you, ma'am," he said, then arose quickly and strode into the hallway, dashed up the stairs two at a time. He didn't hesitate a second. He had never been abovestairs before, but a flashing tail of skirt told him not only her room, but that she had been listening over the bannister as well. Entering not a minute before him, Prudence slammed the door; it was still rattling when he reached it. He pulled it open and entered without knocking.

The long wait and the disapointment had worn his

nerves thin. His voice was loud when he spoke. "If you have something of importance to say to me, Prudence, have the gumption to say it yourself, and don't send your mother to do your dirty work."

She rounded on him, furious. "I said what I had to say to you yesterday. I thought my meaning must be perfectly clear. When a lady returns her engagement ring and tells a man she doesn't want to marry him, anyone but an *idiot* must get the message. As I am clearly dealing with the exception, I will spell it out so that even you cannot misunderstand me. I don't ever want to see you at this house again. We are through, completely, utterly done with each other forever."

"Not quite done! It has apparently slipped your mind that *I* was involved in the engagement as well, and I deserve a better excuse for dismissal than that I offered shelter for a night to a friend in trouble."

"Then I'll give you nine or ten or a hundred other reasons! You are immoral, conceited, a liar, a libertine and damned impertinent, sir, to send me threats by my mother."

"I am not a libertine!" he jumped in at once, lighting instinctively on her real objection. "It is a reflection of your mind that you impute lechery to me when I was doing no more than housing the afflicted."

"You ought to have clothed the naked while you were about it."

"She wasn't naked!"

"Next to it. If I had arrived five minutes sooner . . ."

"If you had arrived five minutes sooner, you would have discovered me on the sofa in the drawing room. I had to go into my bedroom to get my jacket."

"Odd you found it necessary to warn Hettie to *get rid of me,* if picking up a jacket was your only business in Cybele's room. Odd, too, you were having a cup of

33

coffee with her, now I come to think of it, with a breakfast tray for two by the bedside."

"That wasn't my idea—the tray! I was in a hurry, and carried my coffee in with me. I only told Hettie to take you away for a minute because I *knew* what you'd think. I know the way your mind works."

"If you had the least conception how my mind works, you wouldn't be wasting my time and your own with this scene. *I* am of the opinion that the position in which I found you allows me no other course than to be finished with you. Any woman in Christendom would say the same."

"It is a sad reflection on Christendom to take this high-handed tone with me. I found you in a very similar position with Mr. Seville at an inn in Reading not so very long ago, and didn't feel it necessary to raise a fuss about it."

"You found me having a cup of tea with Mr. Seville, who was kind enough to help me when Mama took ill. She was lying in the next room, and you *did* make a considerable fuss. You threatened to shoot him."

"I should have! To be in your bedroom at midnight."

"We were both fully dressed, at least. The circumstances were entirely different."

"No, they were very much the same. Seville helped you when you were in trouble, and it chanced he ended up in your room at an unseemly hour. *I* helped Cybele when she was in trouble, with the same result. Also with the same result in both cases of *my* ending up in the wrong, being kicked out as though I were a mutt."

"You are no better than a mutt!"

His body tensed, and a cold anger shook him. "You were happy enough to make use of the *mutt*, however. To use my connections and influence to ingratiate yourself with society, and get your books reviewed in

34

Blackwood's Review. To make an advantageous marriage. What changed your mind, as you apparently recognized me for a cur from the beginning?"

"I thought you had changed, but you can't teach an old dog new tricks, after all."

"You taught me a few, Prudence. I thought you were different from other girls, immeasurably better. I thought we had a relationship of mutual trust and respect and understanding."

"I can't respect a man who doesn't respect himself. To invite that trollop into your house, and us on the very edge of being married."

"She's gone. I took her away."

"Back to the love nest, Dammler? Swallow Street, was it not, where all the ladybirds roost?"

"No, she's gone to stay with some friend on the corner of Conduit and Bond."

"That would be handy for you, with your own new house in Berkeley Square within whistling distance. Chosen with that convenience in mind, no doubt."

"I didn't choose the apartment. Wills arranged it. She's got a job with him in the play."

"Better and better! An unexceptionable excuse to see her every day. That will give society a good laugh, to see your mistress starring in your new play, while the bride sits home, ignorant of the fact."

"She isn't starring, and you are not ignorant of the fact that she has a small part, as I just told you."

"I am not going to be the bride, either, so it's no matter."

"I won't be back, Prudence," he said, studying her with a carefully controlled expression. "If you send me away now, I won't *ever* be back. Even a mutt will grovel only so far."

35

"I'm glad to hear it. Pray don't slam the door when you go out."

"This is the end then."

"The end, finis, curtain. Make a nice bow."

He made no bow, but turned and walked briskly out the door, giving it a good slam behind him.

She was half glad it was irrevocably over and done with, and wholly sorry that it had ended this way. Her next step was to reconsider their argument, and find an insult in every word he had uttered. To imply she had *used* him to advance herself was unforgivable. He *had* arranged the interview that got her books reviewed in *Blackwood's Review,* but she had not egged him on to it, had been ignorant of his part in it till it was all over. The rest of it was pure fabrication. She had not wanted to travel in his set, he had dragged her into it. As to dredging up the Seville business again! A wealthy gentleman who had asked her to marry him, and later, after she had refused him, had accidentally been staying at the same inn in Reading, and got her a doctor when Mama was poisoned by shellfish. He had been in her room late, and it was unfortunate in the extreme Dammler had come bursting in to insult the poor man, but to suggest there was any impropriety in it was absurd. Talk about a reflection of one's own mind! He was only trying to excuse his own behavior, but it was inexcusable, and he must know it.

4

The summer in London was hot and tiresome. With company thin, Dammler went out only seldom, and when he did so, there was no sign of Prudence. What she was doing he could only guess. He remained in town himself only because of his play in rehearsal. Prudence was not accustomed to the luxury of spending her summers anywhere else than in the city, so that was no added burden. She tried to work on her book, but it went poorly. She had lost interest in virtuous Patience. She wanted a new character, a girl involved in more lively pursuits than going to the greengrocer for her mother. With the past weeks reeling in her head, she wanted a heroine who was involved with the high and mighty. Her sharp eye had been busy to note the foibles of the *ton*, and she longed to give them a trimming down. A girl who came to society with a fresh eye would do the thing as she wished to do it. Someone like herself, who had not grown up amongst them, and thus saw their behavior for what it was.

Almost she felt it a duty to point out the immorality that ran rampant amongst those she had lately been associating with. Adultery was a way of life with them, with gambling, debts and dissipation all a part of it. Yes, it would make an excellent, instructive book. When she sat down, the words seemed to come of their own accord. Hettie was there, leading her young relative astray, but she was careful to give no similar physical characteristic to her book people when she wrote from life. The relationships were changed. She made herself the daughter of a minister to give the girl a little extra whitening, and to insure the character's not being taken for herself. She eliminated her mother but revived her own father for the minister. Dammler she elevated to a duke (so he couldn't say, if he ever found out, she had lowered him). She also gave him blond hair, while his world travels were limited to a stint in France. Never having been there, she knew only its reputation and didn't feel the rest of the world could possibly outdo it in infamy. Not a mention of his being a poet. Mr. Seville became her real hero, for of course her heroine must have a happy ending, and the duke be delivered of a suitably bad fate. She equivocated between the gallows and Bedlam, settling in the end for his sheering off to America, for even in fiction she couldn't quite bear to kill him. As she wrote, she had uphill work making Seville interesting. He became a shadow figure, with the villain taking over as the central character. Too close to her work, she was blinded to this flaw in the story, the playing down of the supposed hero. To increase the difference between the villain and heroine, the lady was endowed with every imaginable virtue.

It was a wonderful diversion for her. She could think of Dammler all day long, twisting him into a form that was easy to hate, but the real Dammler had no such diversion. He was frustrated, bored, and still ferociously angry. To call him a *mutt!* It was infamous. Yet as he reviewed his past life, it didn't seem so far fetched. What had he, born to wealth and position, accomplished? A thin volume of inferior verse, and a play that was presentable only because he had put some of Prudence's wisdom into his heroine. His life had been as hapless and promiscuous as a dog's. She was right, as usual. The play progressed satisfactorily, the rewriting all done by early August. He thought of going to Longbourne Abbey, but to go alone where he had thought to go with Prudence—he couldn't face it. When Hettie invited him to her place in Surrey, he accepted.

Hettie, a confirmed socialite, had no thought of going alone or only with her nephew. She had a host of friends joining her at intervals for varying lengths of time. She took pains to invite several eligible young ladies to amuse Dammler, and with a mischievous chuckle, she also invited the Malverns. Lady Malvern was reputed to have been Dammler's mistress. She didn't know whether it was true, but it was certainly possible, as he had spent sundry holidays at Finefields with the lady and her husband. Had finished off his second batch of cantos there, in fact. The alacrity with which the invitation was accepted tended her to think there was more than friendship between the two.

Her plans bore little fruit. Dammler soon fell into the routine of walking off into the park or woods with his notebook right after breakfast and staying there for the greater part of the day. What he was writing she didn't know, but it seemed to keep him in good humor, so that he helped her entertain the company in the evenings. He discussed his work with no one. Occasional notices appeared in the London papers of the departure and arrival of guests at Lady Melvine's place. Such celebrities as Lord Dammler and the Malverns did not go unannounced.

"I see Lady Melvine has got the Malverns to go to her for the last half of August," Clarence said, sipping his tea one fine morning. "And the Swazies. I expect you know all these folk, eh, Prudence?"

"I know of them," she replied, clenching her jaw to control her anger. Lady Malvern! He had gone running back to her!

"A pity she didn't ask us. I would like to get away from the sweltering heat of the city for a week or two. But they will all be back in September. All our friends will be turning up one of these days. I confess I miss them."

To call these people "friends" was another of Clarence's delusions. To hear he expected to continue association with them filled Prudence with forebodings of despair. Clarence would not like having all his vicarious glory snatched from him. He had remained civil to her all summer long, but if September did not return him to his recent pinnacle of fame, he would soon turn on her. Uncle was capable of wretched behavior under the strains of deprivation. She tried to give him a hint that things would be different. He wouldn't hear of it.

"Pooh—Dammler ain't the only fish in the sea. Glad you turned him off. I always thought you would have done better to take Seville. There was a man knew how to treat a lady. Called in Knighton when Wilma took sick at Reading. That was well done in him."

"Mr. Seville is married now, Uncle," she reminded him.

This was too much reality to quibble with. "So he is. To that Scots baroness, wasn't it? Well he had an odd knot or two in him. A foreigner, after all. I didn't like him nearly so well as that Springer lad that hounded your every step in Bath."

"Mr. Springer has gone home to Kent. He does not come to London."

"Just as well. He is nobody, when all's said and done. Do you mind that royal duke that used to trail at your skirts, Prue? York was it, or Kent . . ."

"The Duke of Clarence—I remember him, certainly." She remembered as well that his trailing at her skirts

40

was limited to once standing up with her at one of Hettie's balls.

"That would be something, eh? A royal duke."

"Yes," Prudence said weakly, unable to say more.

"Oh, Clarence, that is looking a good deal too high," his sister told him.

"Aye, so it is. The old king would never let him do it. But we will have Dammler pounding down our door soon, if I know anything." They had gone full circle, right back to Lord Dammler. "What a lad he is. Up to anything. The women are all over him." In this manner he whiled away the summer. He had a few actual activities as well. He visited Stutz for a new pair of coats, dashed off a couple of Rembrandts a week, the dispersal of which consumed a good deal of his time. Not every one of his friends wanted a brown picture in the saloon. His most outstanding activity, however, outshone all of these. It quite wiped Dammler and Lady Melvine from his mind for three days.

He mentioned his plan over breakfast one morning, sliding it in calmly between bites of egg, not to lessen its wonder, but to show how very much he had fallen into his new role as confidant of lords and ladies. "I guess it's time I take a run down to Drury Lane and pick out our box," he said.

Never in his life before had he hired a box for the season. Seldom did he even go to the theatre. He got all the astonishment he craved.

"Oh, Clarence, that will be very dear," Wilma said at once.

"You don't mean you are going to hire a box!" Prudence said, right on top of her mother's exclamation.

There was a good deal of discussion, with Wilma against the extravagant plan and Prudence delighted with it. Clarence was actually interested in no one's

41

opinion but his own, however, and didn't let Wilma talk him out of it. He wore one of his new jackets for the trip down the Strand, sitting on the high perch of his phaeton, and toying with the notion of taking the ribbons himself, a thing he had never dared to tackle thus far. But a man who could hire a box for the season was up to anything, and if the coal carrier had looked what he was about as he came ripping out of St. Martin's Lane, there wouldn't have been a hitch in it. The scratch on the side of the phaeton hardly showed, and the horses weren't hurt in the least.

The summer seemed to them all to last a very long time, but at last it was over. When September rolled around, Prudence, who had done little but write the past six weeks, sent her new manuscript to her publisher. Mr. Murray read it with astonishment. It was so very different from her customary work! She, who usually wrote of her own class in an understated way, had tackled high society, and done a successful job of it. It was not as sound a book as she generally turned out. The characters were thin, superficial except for the two main protagonists, and these he soon recognized for herself and Dammler.

He came around to Grosvenor Square to discuss the matter. "Are you sure you want to go ahead with this, Miss Mallow?" he asked with diffidence. He was dying to publish it. It would be an immediate hit, but Dammler after all was still his major writer, and it wouldn't do to antagonize him.

"Why else do you think I wrote it?" she asked. "You forget I am not one of the privileged few who write for my own amusement. I write for money, and I happen to be in need of funds." Her trousseau, hanging idle in a closet, had rendered her bankrupt. She had actually had to borrow from Mama to buy a new set of pens.

"It seems a little personal is all I meant."

"Personal? How can you say so, Mr. Murray? There are no real people in it. Just my imaginary characters, as usual."

"I think your Duke of Guelph has just a little something of your ex-fiancé in him?" he asked.

"I could have written of an aged humpback and it would be taken for Dammler at this point. That can't be helped."

"Yes, but you haven't written of an aged humpback; you have chosen for your hero a handsome young peer."

"Guelph is not the hero!"

"Well—major character—you know what I mean. I am not at all sure it is wise." But as he thumbed through the manuscript, picking out lively scenes, dialogues sparkling with witty repartee, he felt a very strong urge to get it between covers. If he didn't, someone else would. Colchester, now, would die to get his hands on it.

After a moment's consideration he suggested, "What do you say we put it out under a *nom de plume?*"

"An anonymous gentlewoman, you mean?"

"Your anonymity would not last long. A name, I think, would be better, and we'll invent a biography for her."

Prudence felt just a twinge of concern when Murray had so quickly found out her stunt. She had gone a little far, she admitted, and leapt on the idea of hiding her authorship. "Excellent! Who shall I be?"

"You've made your heroine a minister's daughter. Why not make yourself the same? A Miss Brown would lend a nice touch. Plain, without quite giving it away for an alias by using Smith or Jones."

43

"Why not Miss White, as I have made her so pure? Miss Mary White. How does that strike you?"

"You've called your heroine Mary. Let's make it Jane."

"Jane White. I like it excessively. As bland as pap—it doesn't give a single hint of anything."

"Done! I shall launch my new authoress as soon as possible. I've just got a manuscript from Dammler," he went on.

She was on tiptoes to hear all about it, but could not sink so low as to show her eagerness. "What is it, poetry, a play, what?" she asked nonchalantly.

"Poetry," he replied, a little ill at ease.

"Another batch of the cantos?"

"No, sonnets. A collection of love sonnets."

"Ah, he has got his summer's experience on paper already, has he? There will be a good profit for you, Mr. Murray."

"I expect they will do very well. They are excellent, in my estimation. Perhaps you'd like to look them over when I have the proofs ready?"

"I can wait till they're in the stores. I am not that interested in Lord Dammler's work any more. Now, about my *Babe in the Woods,* sir, it is not a large book. I think two volumes will do for it?"

"Yes, there's not enough here to require three volumes this time."

"I hope you don't mean to pare down my money accordingly? I am very short at the moment."

"Same price. I'll send the cheque right over, if you're short. And you won't tell anyone who wrote it?"

"Not unless it is a runaway success," she returned impishly.

"It will be that. It's Dammler I'm thinking of, actually."

44

"Tell him what you like. Tell him Jane White wrote it, and has since entered a convent. That is bound to divert any incipient interest he may have felt in the authoress."

"He won't take the idea it's about him if he believes it was actually written by someone he doesn't know." John Murray, not so very intimate with the day-to-day doings of his two favorite writers, had no way of knowing Dammler would recognize a phrase of his own on every page.

"He is convinced he is the hero of my other book, *Patience,* and won't be looking for himself so soon in anything written by me. But we won't say I wrote this. Meanwhile, I shall go on with *Patience.*"

"Do that. I like the chapters you showed me. If we could bring *Patience* out soon, no one would think you had written this one as well. You did a fast job of it, this time."

"I was inspired."

They discussed printing and finances, and soon Murray was leaving. Prudence sat behind, wondering how soon she might get ahold of a copy of Dammler's sonnets, and realizing her eagerness would be less if she had put him out of her mind and heart as she had hoped she could do. That he had written love sonnets intrigued her. She sat wondering if she could guess from the poems whom he was writing to. The images of Cybele and Lady Malvern were in her mind, along with those names visiting Hettie to which she could put a face. She was required to chase out the scampering thought that there might be one or two to herself. She was becoming as foolish as Uncle Clarence, to think he would write love poems to a lady who jilted him, and called him a mutt.

There had never been any formal cancellation of the

45

wedding in the papers. Clarence couldn't bring himself to do it, and Prudence was so distracted she forgot all about it. It devolved on Mrs. Mallow to send out individual cards telling the news. As a result, those returning to town in the fall, those who had not been invited, were in some little confusion as to what had happened. Prudence received some few calls from the more elevated persons she had come in contact with through Dammler. Even a few invitations were extended to her. Accepting them smacked of using him, the worst of his charges in her view, but turning them down augured such a tedious autumn that when Clarence set a pen in her fingers and commanded her to accept—on his behalf as well as her own—she snatched at this poor excuse, of pleasing Uncle, and did as she was told. She was only human flesh and blood after all; she wasn't Jane White. There lurked as well the unworthy hope that she would see Dammler at some of these do's. She had tried her very best to root him out of her heart, but like a mint plant or an ivy, the last corner of root refused to be eradicated, and flourished without a bit of encouragement. Two consecutive evenings she made a careful toilette, accepted Clarence's delighted escort to *ton* parties, and spent the better part of her time scanning the crowds for Allan, without any luck.

Clarence was pleased with her. Dammler hadn't yet come breaking down her door, but new names were learned, new faces to bow to on the street and mention to his cronies were assimilated. There was enough novelty in peeking around corners of fashionable homes and informing the owner she had a fine Canaletto or Rubens there to keep him happy. Each new day brought another card or two to his door, and there was the thrill of trying to remember what the sender looked like, and wondering whether the address mentioned was the big brick place on the corner, or the little dab of a spot next it. Often the phaeton was harnessed up to check on these matters before the invitation was accepted. Clarence Elmtree didn't mean to honor just any old place no bigger than his own with his presence.

The third outing brought Prudence face to face with her quarry. She wore one of the gowns from her trousseau, and wondered if Dammler recognized it. It was a gold silk gown he had informed her would set off his late mother's topaz and diamond necklace to a nicety. It was set off on this occasion, however, by no more than a short string of amber beads belonging to her own mother. Even before she and Clarence got into the hall, they saw him at the doorway to the main saloon, standing with two gentlemen and a matron. His face was brown and relaxed; he looked younger, more handsome than she remembered, with just that tip of a brow tilting up to lend him a slightly raffish air. As usual, he was talking away, gesturing with his well-shaped hands, leading the conversation, laughing and joking. ". . . said he hadn't seen hide nor hair of his wife in six months, so I took him home, and sure enough, there she was," he finished up some story, being outrageous as usual. Then as his listeners espied Prudence and her uncle approaching, their glances went to her in an expectant way.

Dammler looked across the hall and saw her. The smile left his face. The group fell silent, watching to see what would occur as a result of this first public meeting since the break. For a long moment, nothing happened but that they stood staring at each other, each overcome by the dreadful premonition of being about to be cut dead. Clarence's roving eye lit on Dammler at this moment, and he bounced forward with his hand out, leaving Prudence behind.

"Well, well, so you're back, eh, Dammler?" he asked happily, not yet daring to use the "Nevvie" that longed to come out. "We have been scanning the papers every day to see when you would get here. Had a good holiday with your aunt, I trust?"

"Very good, thank you," he answered politely, his eyes sliding past Clarence to the niece, who cringed to hear her uncle blurt out the devastating truth, the lowering fact that they had all been following his moves, awaiting his return. Prudence saw the astonishment clearly on his face, the little widening of the eyes and lift of the brows.

Clarence forged on with the welcome. "Good for you. There is nothing like getting away from the heat in the dead of summer. We would have been happy to go somewhere ourselves, but Prudence was scribbling away like crazy, and has got a new book sent off to Murray."

This news was to have been suppressed at all costs. How had she not thought to warn Clarence of it? But he seldom spoke of her work; she hardly realized he knew she had given Murray the manuscript.

"Indeed?" Dammler asked with the quickest of interest, using it as an excuse to approach the forbidden lady. He took three steps towards her, and executed a bow. "You have had a fruitful summer, I take it?" he asked her, careful to keep the talk impersonal.

"Not so fruitful as Uncle would indicate. I have not finished *Patience* yet."

"Nonsense. Murray took a great box of papers away two weeks ago or more," Clarence threw in. " 'Another book, eh, Mr. Murray?' I asked him, for I was coming in just as he went out, and he said, 'The girl's a demon for work. At this rate, she'll outrun Burney. Frances Burney, he meant. She's a writer, too," he told Dammler, who had no need to be informed of the employment of a

48

good friend and the most famous female writer in the country.

Prudence was sure the fat was in the fire, but soon realized Allan was hardly listening to her uncle babble on. He was looking at her, not hearing much of anything, she thought. "I have been writing too," he told her.

"Murray mentioned it. I am eager to see your sonnets," she answered in confusion.

"I'll bring you a copy when they're ready—if I may?" he asked. He sounded uncertain, but there was a definite trace of conciliation in him.

She was so relieved to discover he was not angry, not dead set against her, that she forgot all her good resolutions and answered, "That would be very nice."

"You must give me a copy of your new work, as well. When will *Patience* make her bows?"

"Oh, I have not finished *Patience* yet," she told him quickly.

"What book is it Murray has then?"

She hesitated. She could not like to lie outright and say he had none, but liked even less to own up to what she had done. It seemed suddenly a gross thing, to have painted this forgiving man as an absolute monster. Clarence had wandered off to meet those Dammler had abandoned, and without him to overhear her, she said, "You must not put total reliance on my uncle's words. He sometimes is confused."

"Was he confused in thinking you had been looking out for my return?" he asked.

It was as close as he could come in public to asking whether he were still in the doghouse, where a mutt, of course, belonged. "Not totally confused," she answered, embarrassed pink, but happy to see the subject of her new work being dropped. To ensure that it not come up again, she asked quickly, "I assume *Shilla* will be opening on schedule? I look forward to seeing it."

"I'll send you tickets," he said at once. "I would be happy if you would share my box. It is a good one. You recall, perhaps, its location?" As they had gone together to select the box in the halcyon days of their engagement, this statement was weighted with more meaning that a bystander might think.

This offer went well beyond mere conciliation to plain pursuit. Unfortunately, she was required to put him off. Clarence, so thrilled with his box for the season, had got together a party for the first performance, of which Prudence was the main star. She told Dammler of the plan, softening her refusal in a way that she hoped would give him no offence, for in her heart she wanted to go with him. She was *Shilla*—what more fitting than that she see the play with the author, in *their* box?

Her prolonged and confused explanation caused a wary light to come into his eyes. It sounded to him more like an excuse being concocted as she went on than a reason. But still he pressed on with his pursuit. "I'm having a party later at our—*my* new house on Berkeley Square. I have moved in and am refurbishing it. I'll send you a card. May I hope to see you there?" he asked, a little less friendly than before.

"Oh, but we are going with Sir Alfred and Mrs. Hering," she explained.

"The whole party will be invited, of course."

"In that case, I expect Uncle will be delighted," she answered with relief that some plan had at last been worked out.

"Prudence!" he said, shaking his head with a rueful smile. "You know it is not *Uncle's* presence I am trying to insure. *You* will come?"

All his words, the spontaneous mention of "our" house, the reversion to calling Clarence "Uncle"—all sounded miraculously like a resumption of the pre-rupture status, and though she had adamantly assured herself all summer she would have none of him, she found her heart beating with wild gratitude. "Of course," she said.

A slow smile formed on his lips, and his eyes were happy. She had seen him look so dozens of times, most often just before he kissed her. He didn't say a word, or have to. She knew what was in his mind.

Clarence, watching them jealously, figured two minutes was long enough for a swift worker like Nevvie, and returned to the attack. Dammler, in his eager resolve to reinstate himself, told Clarence the plan of the party at once. Clarence was all magnanimity. "We will be sure to go. Don't worry I'll let her wiggle out of it. She'll be there if I have to drag her."

"He won't have to *drag* you, will he, Prue?" Dammler asked with a warm, intimate smile. She was back to Prue, and the reconciliation was off to a flying start.

She even dared to make a joke. "I sha'n't put him to the expense of a team of wild horses. The bays he got for his high perch phaeton wouldn't be up to it."

"Ho, they are up to anything. Sixteen miles an hour," he exaggerated, remembering the magical number always quoted for a pair of prime goers, though his own sedate team had hardly exceeded six.

"Well, enough shilly-shallying. Let us get on into the hall and see what sort of a shindig it is," Elmtree said, rubbing his hands in anticipation. "I see the Castlereaghs are here. She grows an inch wider every week. I'll speak to him about that new bill he is pushing through." This was the most arrant nonsense. He had not yet scraped an acquaintance with the foreign minister, and had no more notion what bills were in progress than he had of metaphysics, but he knew what he heard others say, and liked to say the proper things.

"I'll see you later then," Dammler said to Prue. Just as she turned to follow her uncle, who set a hot pace in the pursuit of the mighty, he grabbed her hand. "I believe I overlooked complimenting you on your gown. Very elegant." He looked pointedly at the amber beads, saying nothing about topaz and diamond necklaces, but his quizzing smile told her what was in his mind, and her confused 'Thank you," let him know she understood.

Somehow, he didn't see her later, not at close range in any case. She had as many partners as she wanted, but she didn't once have the one she wanted. Dammler danced with a great many girls, including Lady Malvern. He twice smiled at herself, and three times looked as though he were heading in her direction, but once another gentleman beat him to the draw, and twice he was waylaid before he made it. When she and her uncle went home, they had not exchanged another word. She could not be sure Dammler's unusual effervescence at the party had anything to do with herself, but he had been much friendlier than she had expected.

5

Clarence's talk over breakfast was all of Dammler, his being after Prudence again, the post-play party. Mrs. Mallow cast a fearful look on her daughter. She said no words, but the look was enough. *Don't do it!* the look said. Don't get involved with him again, to have your heart broken. "Did you stand up with him?" Wilma asked.

"No, I didn't."

"That's good."

"He didn't ask me."

"I see. He is just being friendly then. That is best."

"Friendly?" Elmtree leapt in. "He couldn't get next or nigh her for the rush of black jackets."

Prudence didn't think it best at all, nor did she think that was the way affairs stood between them. She fully expected to see him at the door that same day, and so, of course, did Clarence. Miss Mallow said not a word of this, but her uncle pulled out his turnip watch a dozen times between ten and eleven, wondering aloud each time what was keeping him. When he still was not battering down the door at eleven-thirty, Clarence could control his eagerness no longer, and had his high perch phaeton called out to go scouting down Bond Street to look for him. Dammler did not come that day, nor the next, nor any day that week. The cards for the party arrived, to be stuck in a corner of the saloon mirror for pointing out to callers.

As day succeeded day, Prudence reviewed the meeting for the hidden cause of his neglect. He had called her Prue, had said *our* house, had called Clarence Uncle, and his smile had been warm, but on the other hand he had danced with Lady Malvern and had not danced with herself. It began to look as though he were playing some nefarious game of cat and mouse. Why did he not come? Was it to be no more than friendship between them, after all? Was this the polite way of smoothing over a broken engagement when two persons were likely to go on meeting? He was redoing the house—would it not be appropriate for him to consult with her if there was a possibility she was to share it with him? Dammler's taste, to judge by his apartment, was a little garish. She had no wish to spend the rest of her life in a saloon that boasted no sofas, but required the inhabitants to be seated on backless ottomans, with the only tables so far below hand level that setting a teacup down was an inconvenience.

She tried to find face-saving excuses for his absence. Impossible not to remember he had a play in preparation—with Cybele in the cast. He would be spending a good deal of time at the theater. Was it Cybele that kept him so busy he couldn't find half an hour to call? As to his host of other friends, she could not but wonder if Lady Malvern were not seeing him.

Dammler was spending his time more innocently than she could have imagined. Between the play, the proofs of the sonnets to be read and corrected, the house to be got ready and new servants to be interviewed, he had hardly a minute free. What minutes he had were passed in restraining himself from running to Grosvenor Square, where he was by no means sure of his reception. Prudence had been friendlier than he dared hope. The rancor was spent, but there had been no eagerness in her welcome. She had made excuses not to join him in his box, had been particular to show him she went to the party to please Clarence, and had not offered him a copy of whatever it was she had given Murray. What could it be? She was open to further advances, but they would be careful and seemly. No eager puppy trotting back with his tail wagging this time. Meanwhile he prepared the house with a lavish hand, in a way he hoped she would like. The coup de grace was to be the book of sonnets. When they were bound, he would take her a copy and let his poems do the job of courting for him.

He was happy with them. Sitting out in the meadow with the warm summer sun beating on his shoulders, he had gone over all the days of their meeting and friendship that had ripened into love. The poems were an unabashed tribute to her, and they were good. The best thing he had done. He knew it before Murray told him. They would tell her in a civilized way what he felt, but couldn't put into words. When he spoke, his tongue ran away with him. It was his besetting fault, that tongue. In the written work he had pared away the excesses and left the essence. She would recognize in them allusions to herself that would pass for generalizations to others, but she would know they were for her. A note in her own particular copy would confirm it. He counted heavily on the efficacy of poetry to appeal to a lady of literary leanings. By a great pressure on his inclinations, he waited for the auspicious moment to approach her, after she had read and digested them.

For the meanwhile, he had plenty to do. A more concrete appeal to her hedonism, a quality which was in fact lacking to her, was the care taken for the redoing of their mutual study in the new house on Berkeley Square. A pair of desks were found, his own having by legend, probably false, been used by Alex-

55

ander Pope, whom he idolized, and hers by Madame du Barry. He had the walls lined with shelves, which were in turn lined with his books, with the requisite two rows left for her few volumes. Pictures, chairs, drapes and the necessary pieces were also chosen with care, as he envisaged many happy hours spent there. He had arranged the desks so she would have a view of the garden, and he a view of her.

When his sonnets came off the press, he got the first copy and inscribed it, after careful thought, to her using the words, "For Prudence, my inspiration, with love from Allan." He would have put more, but wished to express the thought without becoming maudlin. The copy was placed on Madame du Barry's desk, waiting for her.

The night for the opening of *Shilla* finally came—one of the opening salvos of the season. The play was an immediate success. Sitting in Clarence's box, Prudence's cheeks were flushed as she recognized her own sentiments, even her own words, being flung into the theater to be received with rapture. It quite went to her head. Lest the listeners not realize Clarence could have read it all long before had he wished, he decided he had done so, and occasionally reached across Mrs. Hering to inquire, "He has changed that bit, I think?" of Prudence. He laughed and clapped at all the right places, like everyone else, only a few seconds after the others, and several times discovered amusement where no one else did.

During the intermission he was busy hobbling over to acquaintances to ask, "We will be seeing you at Dammler's party after the play, I fancy?" and was *aux anges* when the reply was a jealous negative. He hadn't had such a night in his life before. The expensive theater box had been a sound investment. Next year he

56

would get a better one—closer to the royal family, and hang the expense. He even enjoyed the play, especially the crowds of fillies all with their black hair and funny looking outfits.

"There is a dashed pretty young thing—the one in the pink," Clarence said to the company at large. Prudence had been spending a good part of her attention to search out Cybele, a job made nearly impossible by the black hair of all the girls. Training her glasses on this particular one, she discovered it to be Cybele. She had no lines to say, but did her little dance with her hips swaying very convincingly. At one point she was the last to leave the stage, having a flirtation with the Mogul. Clarence leaned forward to get a better look at her. "I would like to paint her," he said. "An excellent subject. She would be no trouble at all."

At length the performance was over, Dammler was taking his bows, and Prudence thought—it was hard to be sure—that he looked in her direction. She was so proud she wanted to burst. The cream of society was on its feet applauding him. She marveled that she had actually spurned an offer of marriage from this man, who seemed at that moment the most desirable man in the world. How had she been so foolish? The doubts of the past months were clapped and cheered away amidst the uproar in the theater. She could be the hostess of his party this night of his triumph had she wished. Lady Dammler, standing beside him, secure in her future, bathed in the glow of his achievement. Instead, she was to go as a mere guest, and grateful even for that, to the house bought for her. A hundred regrets swirled in her brain, a thousand fears she would not have a repeat chance, and as many resolutions to grab the chance if it offered—if it was not too late. Too late! Surely the saddest words in the language.

Once at the party, she realized she was not just one guest, but a very special one. Allan had claimed the saloon would not hold more than fifty comfortably, but there were close to four times that number of people milling about within various rooms—writers and politicians, ambassadors and dukes, even a royal prince or two, but when she entered she felt she was the one he had been waiting for. She knew him well enough to read his thoughts by his mobile face. A look almost of peace descended on his features when he took her hand. He said no more than, "Hi, Prudence. Glad you could come." The eyes said the rest. He made the rest of the party welcome, then turned back to her. "How do you like the house?" he asked. She had thought it would be the play he inquired about.

"It looks wonderful," she complimented, drawing her eyes away from him to glance at newly done walls, new furnishings, new mirrors and huge tubs of flowers everywhere. The place had been old, poorly furnished. He had had it refinished from ceilings to floors.

"I hope you like the way I have fixed it up?" he asked. Did she imagine the nervous tone in this question. She read volumes into the platitude. What should it matter what she thought of it if she were to spend only an evening here as a guest at a party? "No oriental splendor, you see. The ottomans and hassocks all done away with. Good old Sheraton and Hepplewhite. Hettie gave me a hand with it. I left the black and white marble entrance floor. You said you liked the patterned floor."

Not too hard to read meaning into this remark. When he went on to point out the red carpeting on the stairs, he was as well as saying the place was hers. He had already told her he thought red carpeting a trifle nouveau riche, but she had proclaimed it of particular appropriateness to herself in that case, and if he had put in red carpeting, it was not for his own pleasure.

"It's bright as afternoon in here," Clarence said, frowning at this phenomenon.

"Gaslight," Dammler explained aside. There were other guests waiting to be welcomed, but he held on to her hand a moment longer. "I want to show you the study later. I have something for you there."

In her mind she felt it must be the engagement ring, and went off into the main saloon with a heart that was in flight. It took a little plummet when the first face she saw was Lady Malvern, talking to Hettie, but when Hettie made an excuse and fled right to her side, she rallied. Hettie and Dammler were as close as peas in a pod, so that this distinction was not negligible.

"Well, Prudence, nice to see you again. Are you satisfied with the job we have done on the house?" she asked eagerly.

"Dandy. Just dandy," Clarence answered for her. "Gaslight—I like it excessively. I am thinking of installing it myself." The thought had flashed into his head the minute he saw the bright illumination of the place. Here was a step up on Sir Alfred, and how it would show up his paintings! The brown paintings required a better light than his orange and blue da Vincis had.

Hettie nodded at this praise, but her eyes rested on Prudence. "It's lovely. Very rich," she answered, her glance running from freshly-painted walls that threw the embossings into relief, to silk window hangings, to chandeliers throwing off a million prisms.

"Not too rich for your taste, I hope? Allan vetoed gilt lamps. I tried to talk him into velvet settees, but he insisted you prefer brocade. Done in *blue,* you see," she added, blue being well established as Prudence's preferred color.

59

"Charming," she replied, coloring up noticeably.

"He hasn't shown you your desk yet?" Hettie went on, with a mischievous twinkle. She wore a puce turban topped off with a pair of pink ostrich plumes, tethered with a hideous garnet pin.

Miss Mallow replied, all afluster, that Allan was to show her the study later. "You will like it I think. He got the desk from France—beat me to it, and it was I who heard it was up for auction. But I don't begrudge it to you. You will put it to better use than I would. I never write a word if I can help it."

The desk—was that then what he had got for her? She was disappointed, but it was impossible to fall into actual depression with so much singular attention being showered on her. The desk, surely, was not to be carted off to Grosvenor Square. She was to use it here, under his and her own roof.

The party necessarily began late, after the play, and it was well after two before Dammler, busy seeing to his guests and of course receiving many congratulations, managed to slip away to Prudence's side for a moment. Hettie was showing some people through the downstairs chambers, and Prudence had attached herself to this group, curious to see how the place was done up. Suddenly he was at her elbow, taking her arm. "Would you like to see the study now?" he asked. She must be imagining that trace of uncertainty, shyness, in him. "I locked the door to keep out the throng. My study is sacred. At Hettie's place last summer a souvenir hunter waltzed off with one of my sonnets. But I had made a copy of it, so it was no matter. It's this way."

He led her off from the others, pulling a key from his pocket to open the door. It was dark within, and he busied himself lighting the gas lamps.

"Uncle is very impressed with your gaslight," she said. "He speaks of installing it at home. You'll bankrupt him, with so many luxuries to have to compete with."

The room sprang into illumination, showing her the pair of desks, sitting at right angles. She suppressed a gasp, but it was not with the pleasure or admiration he expected. On the corner of his desk, right under her nose, sat her book *Babe in the Woods*. She didn't have a copy herself yet, but the title and author's name were easily legible. Dammler, gone to pick up his own sonnets, had been given one of the first copies by Murray. She looked away, her face a shade paler, then darted a fearful look to Dammler, who was regarding her steadily.

"You don't like it," he said, disappointed. More than disappointed, dejected.

She felt a wretched traitor, and in guilty confusion forced herself to look around the room, hardly seeing any of his careful work. In her mind's eye the green volume loomed larger than the whole house. "It's very nice, elegant."

He looked on, unconvinced. If she really liked it, she would be making some joke about her own spartan little cubbyhole of a study. "*Too* elegant?" he asked, anxious to discover the cause of her displeasure.

"No—not at all. It is perfect. And the gaslight will make night work easy, too."

He continued to observe, frowning. It was as close to perfect as he could make it. The rest of the house she had approved, but here, where he had gone to the most pains, she was not only indifferent, she was distressed. It was the lady's desk, he decided. She thought it a presumption. He hastened on to make clear he presumed nothing. "Hettie found this treasure for me in France—heard of it from an agent. It was too good to

61

pass up. I may have it sent home to Longbourne," he said. "It used to belong to Madame du Barry. She was an awful woman, but she had good taste in desks, don't you think? It would be interesting to know what epistles were written here."

"Yes," was all she said. She had been reading too much into his politeness and Hettie's. Nothing had been meant by it. They were only making conventional remarks, sounding like saying more because she had been involved in the discussion of the house and its furnishing earlier.

"Mine, so they tell me, belonged to Alexander Pope. I doubt I'll be able to write a word here, with his shadow hanging over me. He casts a large shadow for so small a man."

"You overestimate him, I think. He is all head and no heart."

"A good balance for me then—all heart and no head." He reached down, to her great consternation, and picked up her book. "Have you seen this one?" he asked.

"No—this is the first I have seen it," she answered, the words truthful enough, but the meaning utterly false.

"Murray gave it to me today, hot off the press. I don't usually read novels except yours and Scott's, but he tells me this one will be the rage. Perhaps you would like to have it?" He started to hand it to her, then suddenly set it down. "No," he went on, "I have something else I want you to read instead. I told you I had something for you." He went to her desk and picked up his sonnets. They were contained in a single volume, bound in morocco leather, a deluxe edition. "With my compliments, Miss Mallow," he said, handing them to her.

She looked at the title, smiling in pleasure, the

62

surprise sufficient to make her forget her chagrin for a moment. "Oh, thank you. I have been looking forward to reading this."

"Open it," he suggested, regarding her steadily as she turned back the cover to read the inscription. She was the happiest girl who was ever miserable. She looked at him with tears swimming in her eyes.

"Prudence!" He took the single step that separated them, and folded her in his arms. "Prudence, forgive me. I was a fool to take Cybele in, a damned blundering jackass, but she doesn't mean a thing to me. No one ever has but you."

She lifted her face to answer, and he kissed her, a long, impassioned kiss till her head was spinning. It was all perfect, just as she had hoped and dreamed, except for the book, the malevolent novel she had dashed off in pique, and that stared at her from the edge of his desk. Oh, if only he had given it to her, if only he would never read it, or hear of it. But already it was out, would be in the stores soon, and the money earned from it partly spent, too, so short as she had been. There was no way of stopping its circulation. She must tell him, make a confession and count on his good nature to forgive her. She felt at this moment he would forgive her anything. "Allan, I . . ."

He looked at her expectantly, and the words stuck in her throat.

"I love you, too," he said joyfully, and kissed her again.

It seemed a shame to intrude on this precious moment with so unpleasant a piece of information, and too soon the opportunity was over. Clarence came barging in on them, thrilled to death to find them in an embrace.

With his most debonair air he proceeded to ignore it by saying, "Don't mind me. I'll be out in a minute and let you get on with it, Nevvie." How sweet, to be able to say Nevvie again!

"Do come in, Uncle. You haven't seen our study. I was just telling Prue my desk used to belong to Alexander Pope. Quite a find for me."

"A Pope, eh? You're flying high. You'll be wanting a throne chair to go with it. Mind you don't turn Roman on us. I see you have got your books all laid out, all ten million of them. Makes a very good impression. Looks very like Prue's study. All that is lacking is a couple of pictures there to set off your little mirror. I'll give them to you. No need to go wasting your blunt on them. I have half a dozen in my new style looking for a home." He looked around critically then said aside to Prudence, "You will be able to fix it up very nicely. A couple of pictures will do the trick."

Dammler just caught Prudence's eye, and they exchanged a silent look.

"So this is where you'll be scribbling up your rhymes, is it, where papal bulls were used to be writ. Lo, how the mighty have fallen."

"Very true," Dammler answered unfazed. "Pope Alexander would turn in his grave to know what base use his desk is to be put to."

"Oh, your verses ain't that bad, Nevvie. I like them excessively. I hadn't heard they had run so short of cash in Rome they were auctioning their pieces off."

"Shall we go on out before we have the whole throng in here?" Dammler asked as he heard Hettie's group approach.

"They are at my heels, are they?" Clarence asked, not at all annoyed with the persistence of his fans. "We had better run along then. I see the crowd is thinning. I'll take you home, Prudence. It is after three, and you will be getting sleepy."

It was himself who was having trouble keeping his eyes open. He was sorry to have to pull himself away, but with the euphoria of having patched up things between the lovers, he did it.

Dammler accompanied them to the front door, thanking them for coming, and assuring them he would go to them the next day. Prudence clutched his book, resigned to leave only because she was so anxious to begin reading it. Tomorrow when he came she would tell him about her own awful book, and *make* him understand.

6

Dammler's party was not over before four. He went into his study for a last look around to see what it was that had annoyed Prudence when first she entered. It wasn't the lady's desk, after all. She still loved him, so it should have pleased her, but it hadn't. Really it seemed to be his own desk that bothered her. Did she want a private study; was that it? His mind ran over possible rooms that could be turned into one, though he particularly wanted to share this room with her. He went to give a last good night to Alexander Pope's desk, with a lingering smile at Uncle's nonsense. The man was better than a joke book.

Absentmindedly he picked up the book, *Babe in the Woods,* and carried it with him upstairs. He always read half an hour before sleeping. As he felt his reading would be little attended this night, he didn't much care what he read. Glancing at the title, he made himself a bet the title was wrongly interpreted. The female author would take it to mean a child lost in the woods, or some more civilized symbol, probably a girl out of her element in society, whereas the true origin of the phrase referred to a person set in the stocks. He read two pages, enough to realize he had won his bet with himself, but as he rather enjoyed the author's style, he read on a little further. A phrase here and there reminded him of Prudence, enough to keep him going. By the end of the first chapter, he had concluded someone was copying her style, using her trick of saying one thing and letting it be known by the circumstances quite another was meant. But not so well done as Prudence, he decided loyally.

The end of Chapter Two made him think that not only her style but a little something of her own story was creeping in, too. Someone, some jealous cat—really there was a viperish touch here that was not at all like Prue—was writing a parody of the two of them, or so it seemed to him. He read on with the keenest interest now, confirming that it was about them. He was finished with Volume One in an hour, as he was a quick reader, and when he laid it down, there was a question on his face. It wasn't possible *Prudence* had written this thing. But how very odd that so many of his own ideas were running around in the book, distorted, placed in a new context to make them worse, but still his own ideas—original ones. He hadn't read far into the second volume without realizing that the perpetrator was none other than Prudence Mallow. Certain passages left not a single doubt. Ideas he had shared with no one but herself, and here they were, coming back at him, word for word. Hettie too—certainly "Lady Maldire" was Hettie, with an assortment of rings replacing her customary excess of brooches.

He was so angry the blood thumped in his temples, and so intrigued he had no thought of putting the book down without finishing it that night, which was already nearly morning. The sun was rising when he laid the second volume aside, his face set in a rigid mask of fury. So this was the mystery of her having given Murray a manuscript and not wishing to tell him about it! This was why she had been distraught in the study— and saying she had never *seen* the book! How she must have been laughing up her sleeve! While he had all but idolized her, writing the finest poems he had ever written in her honor, she had been wallowing in this muck. Making him a laughingstock, and herself a saint. She must have thought she had well and truly lost him, to have pulled this stunt. This was her payment for Cybele, and Cybele was in the book to the life, with her platinum curls tarnished to copper. Her sweet smiles, her joy at winning him back—how to explain that? She'd rather have a real live marquess than mere revenge, perhaps. She had used a pseudonym in case he was fool enough to come trotting back to her. There'd be no going back after this. Even a mutt—how *dare* she call him a mutt!—would not grovel this low.

In his anger he pulled the two books apart and flung them into the cold grate, then fished in after the pieces, reading the loose pages again, with a new shot of anger at every line. He didn't bother with the farce of going to bed. He changed into morning clothes and went to Hettie's a good four hours before she was likely to have her head off the pillow. His message to her dresser was violent enough to insure his being received bright and early this morning. She greeted him from her bed, still wearing her cap and an elegant but garish peach satin jacket, dripping with lace.

"You didn't have to wake me from my sleep to tell me the news. I know you and Prudence are reconciled, love. Just tell me the date of the wedding and let me get back to sleep," she said, rubbing her eyes.

"Wedding be damned! Get into your turban, Het, and you'll be in on the execution!" he said sharply.

She rubbed her eyes again, looking at him with the dawning of a brighter interest. "What has the silly girl done now? Don't tell me she doesn't like the house, after the ten dozen shops you dragged me into to pick out all that stuff."

"It is a matter of the most complete indifference to me whether Miss Mallow cares for my house. After

68

you've scanned this piece of libel you'll see what I mean." He threw the two dismantled books at her, their spines broken, the sheets tumbling out all over the counterpane.

She picked up one of the green covers and read it. "Jane White. Pray, what is a Miss Jane White to us, Allan?"

"Alias Miss Prudence Mallow. Look at it! Look at what she has had the damnable gall to publish! Not only *me,* oh, no, she included *you* in her tirade too, Het. 'Lady Maldire'—that is you. A nice touch, don't you think, 'Lady Curse'? Only, of course, with her usual ignorance of French she has got it wrong. It ought to be 'Maudit' "

"Has she written about me, the minx?" Hettie asked, snatching up pages at random and scanning them for a "Maldire." Like so many fashionable fribbles, she couldn't have cared less what was said of her or written, so long as something was. She found herself soon enough. "Lady Maldire, whose greatest labor in life was to vary the color of her gowns and the height of her lovers . . . Oh!" She looked at him, feigning horror, secretly thrilled to death. She was soon rummaging about in the heaps of paper for more "Maldires," and finding a sufficient quantity of them to keep her happy, reading each aloud to Dammler, who was all but frothing at the mouth.

"What should we do about it?" he asked Hettie, pacing the floor and urging her to get up. "I have a good mind to sue. That would stick Murray with the settlement I expect. Not that *he* will escape scot-free, either. *He* knew what she was up to, well enough, probably urged her on to it. And telling me this was the first work of a new writer! But it's not his fault of course, primarily. This is *her* doing."

"Listen to this, Allan," Hettie said, tittering in pleasure. "This must be Cybele—'His current mistress was noted for the metallic luster of her tresses, and the metallic hardness of her heart!' How horrid! What does she say of you? Who are you in this story?"

" 'Guelph.' The name won't be hard to find."

She scrabbled around through the sheets till she found it. " 'He dabbled in the arts, but his real vocation was lechery.' That is coming it a bit strong. Are you sure 'Guelph' is *you?*"

"Of course he's me! And there's worse than that. I'd like to ring her neck, but strangling is too good for her. She should be whipped at the cart's tail."

Hettie meanwhile had settled against the pillows and was reading merrily, quoting a phrase at him from time to time. "Dammit, Hettie, get out of bed. Come with me and prevent me from killing her."

"Why don't you run along and talk to Murray, Allan? Pick me up later. You can't go storming down her door at eight-thirty in the morning. My God, it's only eight-thirty! I didn't go to bed till three hours ago."

"I should murder him while I'm about it. Not to give me a warning of this, he with my sonnets ready to be distributed. *Love* sonnets to that *creature!* What a jackass I'll look! Publicly declaring my undying devotion while she bastes me and serves me up done to a turn, with an apple stuck between my jaws. I've got to stop him. Yes, you're right. I'll see Murray and slap an injunction on him to stop circulation. Glad you thought of it."

Hettie hadn't even heard him. She was reading and chuckling, trying to sort the pages into order for a proper perusal. Dammler made only one stop before going to Murray. When he entered the office, he was accompanied by the sharpest lawyer in town, but was too incensed to allow this expensive minion speak for him.

"Ah, Dammler," Murray said, rising to greet him.

"I am here on business," Dammler said abruptly. "I have an injunction stopping distribution of my sonnets. I want to serve notice, Mr. Murray, that henceforth you are not my publisher."

Murray, who had been worried for some days, was in no doubt as to what had happened. He had given Dammler the book in a seemingly casual way, hoping to divert his suspicions by this ruse, but clearly it had not worked. "What seems to be . . ."

"Cut line, Murray. You know what this is all about. I want every one of those copies of my sonnets delivered to my home on Berkeley Square. If I hear of so much as *one* in circulation, you'll regret it."

"We have a contract!"

"We *had* a contract. If you're wise you'll tear it up, as I have done mine. Go ahead with circulation and you'll have a suit for a hundred thousand pounds damages for that scurrilous piece of trash of Miss Mallow's you had the ill judgment to publish."

"If I hadn't, someone else would have, Dammler. It's done anonymously. No reason to think anyone will suspect . . ."

"The whole town will know it's me! *You* knew it. The book is out, and I won't have my sonnets on the same shelves as that tripe. Do you understand?"

"It might be possible to get the copies of Miss Mallow's book back . . ."

"Let her have her little joke, but I won'd add to it by having the sonnets out for a comparison of our *styles*."

Murray was not simple enough to think the styles had anything to do with it, and tried once more to talk him around. "Those poems are the best thing you've done, Dammler. The finest poetry I've seen in several years. Surely you're not going to suppress them entirely."

"Come to the bonfire," Dammler said, and stomped from the office, while his lawyer wordlessly laid the injunction on Murray's desk, tipped his hat, and trotted out at his master's heels. He wondered why he had been brought along. It was still only nine-thirty, an unseemly hour to call on a lady, but not too early, Dammler felt, to rouse a vulture. He got rid of the lawyer and went on to Grosvenor Square. He was too impatient to go back for Hettie.

He felt if he had to spar with Mr. Elmtree this morning he might do the innocent old fool an injury. He was relieved on that score at least. Clarence had gone out half an hour since, to tell Sir Alfred about the play and the party afterwards. Sir Alfred had attended both himself, but this didn't save him from the visit. Dammler was admitted to Prudence's study by a servant, and found her sitting over her desk, demure in a dark gown with a white collar, a quill between her fingers, a curl falling over her ear. He had seen her like this dozens of times, hundreds in his mind's eye. It was the main way in which he pictured her, the image a sort of icon. It jarred him, to see her look so sweet, so innocent, and to compare the nunlike appearance with the recent behavior. When she looked up, she smiled and held out her hand to him. He stood a moment looking and shaking his head, as if he would make sense of the senseless.

She observed the strange look on his face, and her smile faded. He had found out, had read it already! "Allan?" she said in a soft, frightened voice.

He felt a weakening stab of love, and fought to control it. "It would be better if you call me Lord

Dammler, Miss Mallow," he said, his voice as cold as ice.

"Oh you know," she said simply. "I wanted to tell you myself first. To explain . . ."

"Why did you not, Miss Mallow? Last night, when I offered you the book and *you told me you had never seen it before,* for instance, might have been an opportune moment. Of more interest to me is why you chose to write such a piece of carrion."

She wet her lips, stinging under the 'carrion.' "I don't know. I was angry I suppose, hurt, when you had Cybele at your apartment."

"Surely *you,* of all people, know very well my real vocation is lechery. You didn't think I would pass a whole night alone!"

" 'Guelph' wasn't really you!" she said at once, recognizing her own phrase.

"He was me! You made the portrait quite clear, just prettying up my face a little, like your uncle who so kindly painted out my crooked eyebrow. I must confess I am in some doubt as to whether that saintly female 'Mary,' prone to vapors and hysteria is *you,* but about the others there can be no doubt, in our or anyone else's mind."

" 'Mary' is not me! You know I don't use real people."

"You used me, Prudence. When I didn't pan out as a husband, you got the next best thing out of me, a character for one of your books."

"I don't know why you always think I am writing about you!" she said, her own anger rising at his sharp attack.

"Do you think I don't recognize my own ideas, my patterns of speech? The best part of that very inferior hack job, if I may say so. I want to thank you. You have managed at one stroke to bring me to my senses. I had

73

you on a pedestal, and I should be eternally grateful you tumbled yourself off before I erected a scaffold and tried to vault to your celestial heights. Tell me, Miss Mallow, for I confess this one point escapes me, if you have such a holy aversion to one of my low principles, why in God's name did you ever agree to marry me?"

"It was just a book—I only wrote it to pass the time."

"You gave it to Murray for publication!"

"I needed the money."

"That, my sainted sinner, is known as prostitution. Cybele's sort is better. At least she smears no one in the process. She uses her God-given talents, such as they are, for man's pleasure. You take a gift—I grant you some slight talent in writing—and use it to persecute your friends. *Ex*-friends! Now, who is worse, you or Cybele?"

She was on her feet by this time. "Allan, I'm sorry!" she said. "I shouldn't have done it." She reached her hands out towards him in an impulsive gesture.

He just swayed towards her, but his anger firmed his resolve. "Well you might be! That's the difference between us, Prudence. I poured out my heart to you in those poems. I wasn't ashamed to tell the world how I felt about you, and you reciprocate by making me a caricature in a satire on love—do it behind my back for money. Hang on to your copy of the sonnets. You have the only one that will survive. You will be deprived of having society laugh at my slavish devotion, but the fact that it may one day be worth some *money* will comfort you."

"What are you doing with the sonnets?" she asked, aghast.

"I have become uninspired. You'll have to jog along on your laurels from *Babe in the Woods*. A misnomer, by the way, but then accuracy is clearly of little account to you."

"If Murray isn't circulating *your* book, maybe he can stop distribution of *mine* as well. No one need know."

"*I* know, Prudence. But then, I begin to understand *my* feelings count for nothing. It is less the snickers of the mob that troubles me than the knowledge that you despise me. You felt like that, and were still willing to marry me. Yes, you would have had me last night had I offered for you, and I thank God I didn't!"

She was battered by so much hate and bad luck. She just looked, wordless, too sunk to explain anything.

"Well?" he asked, in a sharp curt way that was not easy to answer. "Speechless, I see. A pity your communication is limited to the printed word. I shall be looking forward to your next book, to see which victim you choose to perform a vivisection on, and to discover what new virtues you can find to heap on yourself."

He turned to leave and she took a step after him, with some thought of further supplication. He lifted a brow and looked at her with such a sneer her blood ran hot. No more supplicating, like a beggar. "A fine rant, Dammler, worthy of a place in one of your vulgar melodramas, if you haven't purloined it from someone else's."

"I am not often accused of *vulgarity,* ma'am. For that particular talent, I direct you to your own latest work."

"I assumed a linguist like yourself would take the word 'vulgar' at its historical value—'popular,' of the people, but let us not be diverted to a discussion of semantics."

"I expect you mean etymology, and as to *purloining* speeches, the less said of that the better. Take my words out of 'Guelph's' mouth and your novel would be half empty pages. As you have proclaimed poverty as

75

your reason for publishing that thing, it will be pointless for me to sue for damages, but it's what you deserve."

"You're not half as interesting as 'Guelph,' and don't think it!" she said.

He was gone, and she sank down on her chair, her head in her hands, too bruised to think. She felt as if she had been physically beaten. With his tender poems still fresh in her mind, the evidence of a deep and true love, to have to hear this abuse, and to know nine-tenths of it was justified, was too much. She couldn't think straight. She sat on disconsolate, remembering him at the play, with the crowds cheering him, at his house afterwards, showing her how he had fixed it up for her—he had done it for her, even if he hadn't said so. Oh, why hadn't she told him about her accursed book then, in the study? What had possessed her to infer she had never heard of it? Dammler hated a hypocrite worse than anything, and she had been a hypocrite of the worst sort. She mentally abased herself till the first shock of losing him was over.

Only then could she subject his tirade to a rational scrutiny. He had called her a prostitute, a worse prostitute than Cybele, for debasing her *slight* writing talent. Surely that was unfair. What would he know, wealthy beyond dreams, of poverty? What would he realize of trying to keep up appearances on the meager allowance she had? He liked her to look well, and with four parties a week, this required many outfits. Of course she had to sell what she wrote, and if she wrote of him in an unflattering way—well, she hadn't said much that wasn't true after all, and had taken some pains not to make anyone think it was he. To have called the book carrion was absurd. Murray liked it excessively. And what had he meant about the title being inaccurate?

This slur on her accuracy, her writing, was as hard to forgive as anything. He said himself his own stuff was claptrap. The new sonnets were not—indeed, even *Shilla* was pretty good, but she had helped. Her words, her speech patterns as he so grandly called them, *purloined*, half of them, were the best part of it. He had a high opinion of himself to call her book carrion. She went on fueling her anger, to keep despair at bay.

7

Clarence stayed with Sir Alfred for lunch, which was a wonderful relief. Prudence had the opportunity to tell her mother she had not made it up with Dammler, after all. They had discussed it and decided they did not suit, is what Mrs. Mallow was told, and as she had not yet read the infamous book, she believed it.

"It is for the best," the mother said. "That is not to say you need sink into a spinster, my dear. Plenty of gentlemen will take a second look at you now that you are a little known."

"Yes," Prudence said with an attempt at a smile. But would they? Would anyone take a second look at her once it became known Dammler was through with her—not only through with her, despised her. Never wanted to see her again. He was highly emotional, Dammler. In his present state she wouldn't put it a bit past him to let it be known he did not wish to grace the same party as herself. No question which of them would be dropped. She couldn't stand to think of never going out again among interesting people. She couldn't work when she was so upset. If society, too, was to be denied to her, she would run mad. Even as she made these silent remarks to herself, she knew she hid from the truth. She wanted to go on seeing him. If she couldn't marry him, she wanted at least to be able to see him. If he didn't speak to her, she would hear him speak to others. She didn't want to lose even the sight and sound of him.

They had scarcely put down their forks when the

front knocker sounded. She knew it wouldn't be Dammler. He might simmer down some day, some ten light years from now, but he was in too towering a rage to be back so soon. She was surprised to hear Lady Melvine wished to see her. Allan had sent Hettie over to add her insults. So be it. Get it over with once for all, and she wouldn't apologize again, either!

"Hettie, my dear!" she said when she swept into the saloon. Hettie had asked her a dozen times to call her by her name, but the Lady Melvine had a way of coming out. She never really liked Hettie nor felt at ease with her.

"Darling!" Hettie said, arising to embrace her. "What a naughty puss you are!" she gurgled in delight.

It was all right then. Hettie wasn't angry. Certainly Dammler would have told her, so she knew and didn't care. Was thrilled, in fact. "Horrid of me, wasn't it? I quite blush to think what I have done. Dammler is fed up with me," she said brightly. She wouldn't let Hettie run back to him and say she was in despair.

"He is white with rage! I never saw him so deranged. He won't be himself for a week. But *I* think you are to be congratulated. Tell me, Prudence, is 'Lady Alabaster' really Lady Malvern?" She laid aside her kid gloves and settled in for a cose.

"You know I don't work from life, Hettie. If people choose to see a resemblance, it is on their own heads."

"*It is,* you minx! I knew it. You made her too pretty. She doesn't have dimples."

"She has *one,*" Prudence laughed gaily.

"And who is the mysterious 'Pierre'? It's Peter Sotheby, I know it!"

This was the nature of their talk. The characters all had to be straightened out. Hettie felt in her heart Dammler would overcome his fit of pique and be back

79

with Prudence within the week, and she herself was so pleased with the sly puss she had no thought of cutting her. Before leaving, she said, "You remember you are to come to me tomorrow night? My little rout party? No one will be there, but come, anyway."

There was no question of "remembering" a party to which she had not previously been invited, but this little deception was overlooked. "I suppose Dammler will be there?"

"He *was* to be. I fancy he won't show up till midnight to show us how mad he is with you. Your uncle will bring you, I hope? I am in need of a *short* suitor—Gratton is ten feet tall, and I always like to vary their height. Minx! How dare you catch me out at my little stunt?"

"He will be charmed to come," Prudence agreed, knowing there was no fear of Clarence turning down the invitation, and happy to have an escort.

They had all given up on Mrs. Mallow months ago. She had been too long a country lady to feel at ease amidst this new set, and had converted an unwilling heart into an ailing one.

"Good. Now I mean to dash right home and read Volume Two. Allan threw it at me in pieces. I see the shops have it on sale today. I'll pick up a copy on the way home, and you must autograph it for me at the party. *Ciao,* darling!" She waved her fingers merrily and was off.

Prudence felt it was a bit early yet to confront Allan. He would not remain so very angry forever, but if she refused this invitation, she might receive no more. There was one whole day and night to be got in before she could go to Hettie's rout and gauge his temper. She spent it in the same manner as a good part of society, reading her own book that Murray had sent over. It was more cynical than she liked, but it was not carrion. The word was circulated in the magical way of a juicy piece of scandal, and by nightfall of the second day, it was all read, digested, and being discussed with an avid interest. Prudence hadn't the heart to tell Clarence she had been jilted. Let him go on in his dream world; he would, anyway.

As Hettie had warned, Dammler did not arrive at the party till very late. He hadn't intended coming at all, once Hettie told him Prudence "might" drop in, but decided that was nonsense. Was *he* to sit home alone because *she* had acted so badly? Certainly not; he would go, and show her (if she had the temerity to attend) by his indifference that he was unaware of her existence. If Lady Malvern were there, he would take her home. It would please the lady's husband, who liked his wife to be popular with all the rakes. How had that bit escaped the book? Prudence mustn't be aware of it.

His vexation reached a new peak to see Prudence not only there, but the center of attention—and looking lovely, too, in a stylish décolleté gown chosen as part of her trousseau. He feared she wasn't noticing how stoically he stayed away from her for the crowd hovering around her. Constance, Lady Malvern, chatting to her like the rest, after being skewered in that book. Was it possible these people *liked* being paraded publicly as objects of scorn? Were they mad? Was he?

He could hardly have been more irate when the person he ended up talking to was Mr. Seville, her rescuer at the inn at Reading. Next to Prudence Mallow there wasn't a person in London he hated more. "I see our little writer has pulled off a new trick," Seville stated, smiling towards the crowd around her.

"New trick?" he asked in a frigid tone. *Our* little

writer. Damn the fellow for an upstart! Prudence had turned him off—she had at least that much taste.

Seville examined him, sensing his hostility, and changed his tack. "They are saying *I* am 'Mr. Rogers.' All a hum, I daresay."

'Mr. Rogers' was the uninspired name of her uninspired hero. "I daresay," Dammler agreed, yawning behind his fingers.

"He is a nabob at any rate, and they call me The Nabob, you know."

"So I hear."

"You are 'Guelph,' of course."

"Mmm, possibly." His voice had assumed the drawling accents it took on when he disliked his companion.

"Must be you. Everyone is saying so."

Hettie, fearing disaster to see these two together, dashed to Seville's rescue. "Dammler, how late you are. Where have you been?"

"I had to see Cybele," he said, hoping it would get back to Prudence, and having a pretty good idea it would.

"Such fun! I have assembled the whole cast of her book, without realizing I was doing it. Except for Cybele of course. Pity I couldn't have asked her."

"You don't seem to care *who* you ask here anymore, Het," Dammler replied, his scathing eye flickering off her star performer and Mr. Seville, the latter of whom turned and walked away. "It seems a monstrous dull do. I think I'll wander on down to Brooks."

"Nonsense, everyone who is in town is here. And having a grand time."

"Having a good laugh at me!"

"Truth to tell, they are laughing at *her*. Roasting her—all in fun, of course. She made her villain more attractive than her hero; he gets all the good lines."

82

"Fair is fair. It is the *villain* who originally spoke them."

"Constance has asked her to Finefields. Isn't it *insane?* She says it is a good place to write, for you wrote your second batch of cantos there. I never thought I'd see the day!"

"What did she say?" Allan asked, pried by curiosity out of his sulks.

"She said thank you very much, but what had inspired Lord Dammler to such heights was not likely to have the same effect on her."

"Meaning I was carrying on with Constance?"

"But of course, goose! What else?"

"What else indeed?" he asked through clenched jaws, and walked forth angrily to detach Lady Malvern at least from Prudence's circle of admirers. It wasn't too hard to do.

"Constance, my dear, how ravishing you look this evening. Criminally beautiful. There ought to be a law against a woman having violet eyes. I wonder Parliament hasn't gotten around to outlawing them. They have taken away all the other good things."

"Or taxed them beyond the reach of most of us," Hettie threw in, darting a look to Prudence, to see if she were aware of Dammler's move. She was, but gave no indication of it.

"We'll have to smuggle you into our boudoir, like a keg of brandy," Dammler said, bending his head close to Lady Malvern's.

"What are you writing next, Miss Mallow?" one of her court asked her. "Are you doing a sequel to *Babe?*"

"No, something quite different," she answered. "I am tired of that set of characters. They have ceased to amuse me."

"They ceased to amuse the rest of us some time ago,"

Dammler said in his drawling sarcastic voice, ostensibly to Lady Malvern, but pitching his words just loud enough that they might be audible to a sharp listener like Prudence.

"As we are amongst them, you are hard on us, Dammler," Constance pointed out.

"You may understand yourself to be excepted, *ça va sans dire,*" he told her with an intimate smile.

"Why don't you try your hand at a play next, Miss Mallow?" some lady suggested to her.

"I had thought of it, but my best lines are already being shouted from the stage by someone else. Someone has plagiarized me," she answered, never looking within a right angle of the plagiarist, who was bristling with the desire to announce that if *they* were her best lines, she had best lay aside her pen.

"She is writing a book called *Patience,*" Clarence spoke up. He was not far from his niece's side that night. "She has been writing it forever. Didn't dash it off like this last one. This one didn't take her a month."

"One would have thought a week more than sufficient," Dammler remarked, again to Constance, who might have been an empty dress for all the note he was actually taking of her.

Prudence heard all his jibes, and knew they were meant for her ears. She was as angry as she could be, but also strangely exhilarated. She couldn't talk to him, but she could let him know what she thought of him all the same, and proceeded to do it. "I feel the characters in *Patience* worthy of more than a month of my time. *Babe* was a mere diversion, a month's pastime in the dullness of summer."

"To provide us all a couple of hours' dullness with the reading of it, now that autumn is come," Constance was informed.

Before Prudence could reciprocate for this taunt, a flurry was created around Dammler by the approaching of a little group of ladies who wished to compliment him on *Shilla*. They hovered just beyond him, waiting for an opportunity to advance. He smiled and beckoned them forward, nodding at their praise. "Ladies, you may stroke me. I am tame," he told them. "Now before someone has the poor taste to proclaim me a plagiarist, let me announce Dr. Johnson as the source of the *bons mots*. 'The *male* of the species of literary lion doesn't scratch. We leave that to the females.'"

Prudence had the experience of hearing him verbally stroked while the attention was gradually but surely drawn away from herself. "Shall we run along, Constance?" he asked, when he had finished putting Miss Mallow in her place.

Constance proved recalcitrant. She was torn by the conflicting desires of making off with Dammler and insuring Prudence's attendance at her next house party at Finefields. One had to have some women, and she preferred they not be attractive enough to rival herself, while yet adding some amusement to the proceedings. Miss Mallow was eminently suitable on both counts. "I'll be right with you, Dammler. Just a word with Miss Mallow first. You will come to us on that date, Miss Mallow—the weekend of October first?"

"I will be happy to, Lady Malvern, but only providing you promise there will be no other *writers* present. One hates the prospect of talking shop all weekend. One hopes to meet more interesting people than writers. We are an abominably stupid, dull lot."

Lady Malvern was by no means slow, and knew very well it was Dammler she was not to ask. She felt she could have him any time, and rashly promised there would be no other writers present.

"In that case I will be charmed to come."

"And your uncle, too. You will come, Mr. Elmtree?"

"I will be happy to. I'll bring my paints with me—but I trust you won't have any other painters there." This sounded a proper qualification to him, or Prue wouldn't have said it. Prudence looked at him with surprise. There was nothing Clarence would have liked better than to meet a real artist, and it seemed a pity he had spiked his own gun.

"What a strange party you will find on your hands, Constance," Dammler laughed, "if every guest must be unique. Only one lady and one gentleman, mind, and the rest to be made up of the other sexes."

"Hush," she said to him. "Very well, Mr. Elmtree. You will be the only artist, but I hope you have no objection to Canova, the sculptor. He is already invited. He is doing a statue of me."

"Oh a dago!" Clarence said knowingly. "I will like to meet him. I admire the Italians. Leonardo and Michelangelo, a fine bunch of artists. Ask any of them you like. I will be happy to meet them."

Prudence's head sunk on her chest at this absurdity. She sneaked a peek at Dammler to observe how he was taking it. He was preparing some jibe, some setdown. There was an anticipatory smile on his face, and a sparkle in his eyes she could not trust. He just glanced at her, and saw her chagrin, the mute appeal in her eyes.

"Let's go," he said to Constance, and they went off together, arm in arm.

It was of course humiliating to see him leave with this acknowledged love goddess, but at least he had held back whatever Parthian shot he had been readying—she knew it would have been lethal. He was getting himself a little in check. This was madness to spar with him in public; she was bound to come off second best. He had pulled away her admirers in two minutes.

When they went their separate ways home, each had to consider the other's insults, and found enough to keep their ire at a high pitch. Still, Prudence had found him less cutting than she had feared. At least he had not laid down any ultimatums about herself attending parties. It never even occurred to her that she was the one who had done that. Dammler was relieved that no one had jeered at him about "Guelph." Society seemed to be taking the thing lightly enough. He wondered if Prudence was actually so short of money she had *had* to sell the book. He knew she couldn't afford the wedding gown she had wanted, and that he had wanted for her. It must be the very devil to be so short of funds.

8

The two feuding lovers met again a few nights hence at Lord Petersham's ball, one of the first of the season, and always one of the best. Everyone was there.

Prudence's book was still one of the major *on-dits*, but the suppression of Dammler's sonnets was beginning to be talked of, too. Murray had delivered the boxes of copies to the new house on Berkeley Square, but there had been no bonfire. Dammler had all the boxes but one carted off to the attics. One sat in the middle of his study, ruining the effect of all the place's finery. A copy was given to an occasional caller and friend, mostly literary cronies, whom he assured his conscience would view it only as a literary work, with no personal significance. They were all too nice to inquire who had inspired the love poems, and accepted his word that they were to Venus. But when Hettie went along with her largest reticule and absconded with half a dozen copies to distribute to her set, and said quite frankly they were to have been dedicated to his fiancée before they had broken up, there wasn't much secret left in the matter. Anyone with an ounce of ingenuity had read the book and knew all about it.

Prudence went to the ball with her most favored escort, Uncle Clarence, but neither felt it necessary to waste any time with the other after arriving. Clarence had a dashing matron, a Mrs. Peabody, in his eye. He had read and heard enough to know any artist worth his salt had a mistress, and was eager to acquire one. The one he really wanted was the pretty little actress from *Shilla*, an out-and-outer, everyone said so, but there was some little trouble in getting ahold of her. She seemed to be living with old Lord Exxon, which was a matter of mystery to Clarence. He assumed they were relations, but the fellow had been pretty huffy when he went to call, and told him Cybele did not drive out with gentlemen. They were keeping the girl wrapped up tight as a nun. A regular prude she must be, and it was odd Exxon let her run around the stage half naked, in diaphanous pants you could see her legs through. Mighty fine legs they were.

Clarence's courting of Mrs. Peabody left Prudence free to pursue her own ends; the major end she had in mind was to get within earshot of Dammler. She had no real desire to cross swords with him again in public, but she did wish to see how he was behaving. So far as she had seen and heard, he was running after every girl in the city. She found him not difficult to keep in sight. Even when she got stuck in a corner with stuffy old Lord Malvern for half an hour, Dammler came and stood not three yards away from her, turned sideways so that he could have seen her if he had wished, but he didn't once turn his head toward her.

He was with a Miss Grenfell, a pretty young heiress, blond and petite. She was one of the elect who had been allowed to stroke him at Hettie's. Dammler's loud talk was first about her hair. "How attractive to see a blonde with brown eyes. One sees such coloring often in Italy, but in England blue eyes are more common. Too common," he added.

Prudence's blue eyes snapped, but as Lord Malvern was telling her about some political business, she could hardly turn the talk around to Lord Liverpool's eyes.

"Is it true you have written a book of sonnets and

decided not to distribute them?" Miss Grenfell asked, smiling happily at her conquest.

"Yes, it is true. Unlike some people, when I write something unworthy of me, I don't insist on foisting it on the public. Some works are best suppressed."

"I don't know how anyone can write poems, and especially such clever ones as *you* write. I have heard said the sonnets are even better than the others. How I would love to read them."

"So you shall, but you will have to let me take a copy and read them to you myself. They are not being passed around. You see how cleverly I manage to insinuate myself into your saloon, Miss Grenfell."

"I'm sure it is an honor, Lord Dammler. "But I know ever so many people that have a copy. May I not have one?" She went on to reel off a longish list.

After having told Prudence she had the only copy left, Dammler was discomfited at this. "Will you be home tomorrow morning, Miss Grenfell?"

"Oh, yes! Will you come tomorrow?"

"I'll *try* to wait till tomorrow," he told her, leaning closer to her, and looking into her brown eyes, while trying to see in the mirror across the room whether Prudence was watching. As she seemed to be paying not the slightest heed, he was obliged to turn away from Miss Grenfell and discover his old friend, Lord Malvern, in the corner.

"Ah, Harold! There you are. How do you do? Where is Constance this evening? I hope you have not left your beautiful wife home? You know all we bachelors only come to these do's in the hopes of having a waltz with Constance."

"You may be sure she is here. She is off waltzing herself to a shadow with young Fotheringham. Her latest flirt, you must know," the fond husband said proudly.

"Careful, now, you are making me jealous," Dammler chided.

"Oh, we are all jealous of her. She is up to anything. I was just telling Miss Mallow how happy we are she is coming to us at Finefields. I am delighted Constance is beginning to ask some pretty young gels to her do's. She usually asks nothing but old dowds and dowagers, you know."

"She knows how to pick the proper foils for herself, but when Constance is in the room, no man looks at any other woman."

Prudence sat silent, refusing to rise to any of his jibes. It was Malvern who spoke up again. "Mr. Elmtree, Miss Mallow's uncle, is to come, too. You would know him, I expect?"

"I have the privilege of his acquaintance. He is an artist, you know."

"So he tells me. He offered to do me while he is there."

"How nice. You must be careful his niece does not do you as well, Harold," he said, smiling.

"Eh? You don't paint, do you, Miss Mallow?"

"No, I don't."

"I was referring to word pictures. Miss Mallow has been known to give us a portrait in prose. Not so well rendered as her uncle's likenesses, I'm afraid."

Still Prudence said nothing, though it became harder by the moment. "Canova is to sculpt your wife, I understand," she said to Malvern, turning her shoulder to Dammler.

"Lucky man," he said behind her back.

"Yes, he is doing her as Aphrodite, a Greek goddess, I believe."

"The goddess of love," Dammler supplied. "I recently dedicated a volume of verses to Venus myself."

"Oh yes, your sonnets," Malvern nodded. "Constance has a copy. Very nice."

"Everyone has a copy. For an undistributed work, they are amazingly widely read," Prudence volunteered. To Venus, were they? He meant Constance, and he had said they were to *her!* And he had given Constance a copy, too, after telling her she had the only one.

"Constance has a copy. I gave a few to my very particular friends," Dammler admitted.

"So Mr. Seville was telling me. *He* has a copy," Prudence topped him, knowing how much he loathed Seville.

He glowered. "I believe Hettie filched a few and gave them to her friends. I did not give one to Seville."

"Nice chap, Seville. He and the baroness are coming to us at Finefields. He will be there when you are, Miss Mallow. You know him I take it?" Malvern asked, in all his naive innocence of the man's former relationship with her.

"We are old friends. I look forward to having the pleasure of the baroness's acquaintance," she replied very civilly.

She noticed Dammler's shoulders tense, and waited for what outrage he would come out with. "You won't find *his* equal elsewhere. Constance need not fear having a duplicate of him on her hands," was all he said.

"He outclasses us all in gold," Malvern said, misunderstanding the remark, and assuming it referred to the man's wealth, one of the few things Malvern knew of him. "We won't have another baroness in her own right there, either. His wife holds the title herself, quite a rare thing. It was the gold that attracted her to Seville, I expect."

This was a perfect opportunity for Prudence to remind Dammler that despite his digs she had meant to marry him for money, she had spurned an offer from the golden Seville, sought after by a titled lady. She toyed with the wording of it, but decided in the end to let it pass as, it would sound so odd to Malvern. Dammler looked at her, and was surprised at the resignation on her face. Why was she not goading him, reminding him she had rejected Seville. They looked at each other, some question in the air, but Malvern, unaware of it, spoke on.

"Ah, there is Seville now. I'll just say how do you do to him—remind him he is to come to us." He arose and walked away, and Dammler had either to go, too, or find himself alone, face to face with Prudence. He regarded her warily, and she looked back with the same careful expression. She was the first to divert her eyes. He took the empty seat beside her.

Dammler had been arguing with himself the past days that he had been too hard on Prudence. She had said she was sorry, and after he had said some pretty vile things to her, too. The book wasn't really so bad. Everyone was saying the villain was the best character in it. He was tired of making up to girls he didn't care a peg for, just to make her jealous, and Constance was beginning to take the notion he was serious about her. He had no desire to fall into her clutches, but most of all he missed Prue's company. Her desk was waiting in the study. For hours a day he sat at his own, pretending to write, but more often than not looking at the empty chair across from him, wishing she were in it.

When at last he spoke, he used an avuncular tone, to show his lessened hostility without giving a hint of any continued passion. "You're running with a pretty fast crowd, the Malverns."

"Yes, your old set in fact."

"I am better able to deal with them."

"I know it well, but my uncle will be there to protect me."

"Clarence will be busy painting Harold."

"That's a relief."

It was no relief to Dammler. "Leaving you free to continue your *à suivre* flirtation with the Nabob."

"That flirtation was terminated when he got married. Unlike *some people,* I do not consider other peoples' spouses fair game."

"Malvern *likes* you to make up to his wife—insists on it, in fact."

"I trust that even in the Malvern ménage adultery is not demanded of unmarried females. I shall be safe enough."

"You have no conception what goes on there! That is no real marriage between Seville and the baroness, for example. He'll be hanging out for a girl."

"You don't have to feel responsible for me. We're nothing to each other now. I'm twenty-five years old, and can look after myself.

"Nothing to each other? No residue of hatred and disgust remains?"

"I was speaking for myself. Apparently you feel differently."

"I do feel differently!"

He wouldn't be sick with apprehension inside to think of her going to Finefields without him if he didn't still love her. She gave him a reproachful look, thinking he said he hated her. All his recent behavior supported the idea. "I *said* I'm sorry! I would undo it if I could, but I can't." She arose, close to tears. Allan jumped up after her. "And I must say, Allan, I think you are very childish to carry on as you have been, making fun of me . . ."

"That's pretty good, making fun of *you!* What about what you have done to *me!*"

"You have performed a miraculous recovery! Don't let on your heart is broken, and you making up to Lady Malvern and Miss Grenfell and any girl you come across."

"We were not discussing *hearts,* only pride," he answered, greatly relieved that they were fighting, clearing the air to get on with the reconciliation.

"Your pride can stand a few knocks."

"Now I am proud, as well as a lecher and a plagiarist, am I?"

"Yes, if you weren't bloated and consumed with pride, you wouldn't have made such a fuss over my book."

"I should like to know how it is possible to be both bloated and consumed at the same time," he said, choosing the least objectionable subject of argument, the semantic one. Such an argument was almost a form of lovemaking between these two bibliophiles, and the one he felt he had the best chance of winning.

"You have consumed it and it bloated you," she insisted mulishly. She knew less, but was as cagey a ratiocinator as her opponent.

He could hardly suppress a smile. "It's pointless arguing with you," he said, but he felt the point was all but gained. He turned away to consider a more conciliating line of talk. His face was stiff with disapproval, but he was happier inside than he'd been in days.

Mr. Seville chose this inauspicious minute to leave Lord Malvern and advance to Prudence. "I hear I will be seeing you at Finefields?" he said to her.

She knew well enough this was a bone in Dammler's throat, and wished the man at Jericho. "I believe my uncle wishes to go," she replied.

"Lovely. We'll get our heads together and talk about old times."

Dammler was pressing his lips with the effort of remaining still. As things had been progressing so satisfactorily between Dammler and herself, Prudence desired to be away from Seville. She made an excuse and left, rather abruptly.

"We are becoming very high and mighty these days," Seville remarked to Dammler, with a disparaging look after her. They had been fighting, the two of them. The romance was off, and Seville said to ingratiate himself with the gentleman, "You were well rid of her. She'd have got you to marry her if she could. Tried it on me, you know. The likes of her—it was not marriage I had in mind, you may be sure. Nor yourself either, I expect, my lord?"

"I beg your pardon?" Dammler asked in a drawl that would have alerted his close friends to disaster. A pulse in his temple beat; he could feel it. He had hated Seville for several months—had always suspected the fellow was up to no good with Prudence, and this was confirmation.

"Offered her a carte blanche and she had the impertinence to broadcast it as an offer of marriage. Fortunately for me, she declined."

"That's what I thought you meant," Dammler said, smiling with satisfaction, just before he drew back his arm and landed Seville a blow on the nose. Caught unaware, Seville reeled against the wall, while the blood spouted like a small fountain.

The two were in a quiet corner, but the racket made by a full grown man hitting the wall with considerable force alerted those nearby to the interesting scene. A little throng of people gathered around them. "Well?" Dammler asked. "I expect that as you *call* yourself a gentleman, you will demand satisfaction. I am eager enough to kill you that I will accept your challenge, without prejudice, as the legal gentlemen say. Meaning, as I know you are not swift to understand, I do not consider you an equal."

"By Jove!" Seville said, pulling a handkerchief out to staunch the flow. "Not a dueling matter. She is nothing to either of us."

"I say you are a coward, sir. Is that nothing to you?"

There were enough gentlemen of the first stare present that Seville must face up to the inevitable and accept a challenge. "My second, Lord Alvanley, if you will be so kind?" He looked to one of the crowd, a fellow-member of the Four Horse Club.

"Mr. Elmtree," Dammler named his second, not knowing till the words were out that he had chosen as poorly as a man well could. Still, it was better to keep it in the family.

Seville tipped his head back, still with the handkerchief to it, and walked away, with Alvanley at his heels to inquire of him what the devil had happened.

Dammler sought out Lord Petersham to make apologies for the fracas, and escaped with the minimum of fuss. He spoke to Hettie before leaving, asking her to take Prudence home, as he had to see Elmtree.

"Allan, they are saying something of a duel! It can't be true. Have you challenged someone?"

"Seville, but don't tell Prudence."

"Is she the cause?"

"Certainly not! I called him a coward."

"Why on earth did you do such a thing—and at a *ball?*"

"Because he is one, and this is where he happened to be."

"But that is no . . . You can't have just called him a coward out of the blue!"

"No, I saw red—but don't for God's sake tell Prue."

"It *is* about her! It has something to do with Finefields, hasn't it? You forbid her to go."

"How should I *forbid* her? Listen, Het, you'd better take her home before she hears something. There's bound to be a little talk."

"A *little?* My dear fool, there will be nothing else spoken of for a month. How exciting! Come to me as soon as you're finished with Clarence. I don't care what hour it is."

It was late. Elmtree was so delighted with the matter that he went to Berkeley Square with Dammler and stayed for two hours.

"A duel you say? That is very serious, Lord Dammler." He was torn between Nevvie and Lord Dammler, but for such an important occasion he deemed the full title suitable.

"Yes, I consider it serious in the extreme that the man made your niece an improper offer—asked her to be his mistress. I'm sure you agree with me that an insult of that nature could not go unchallenged."

"I do agree! I would have run him through myself if I had had the least notion what he was up to. Sending her a diamond necklace—we ought to have known then he was up to no good. Imagine him taking Prue for such a dasher," he added, half pleased with the thought. He was coming to see a mistress was not an outcast in this high society, but had not yet tumbled to it that the mistresses were from the ranks of married ladies, or if single, they made no claims to respectability.

"It is of the greatest importance that he be made to

pay for it. It is the only way her reputation may be saved. You may imagine what would be thought if he were to spread this tale around town with impunity."

"She'd be a byword. But you will not like to involve yourself in such a scrape—a lord. Of course you are to marry her—that makes it eligible for you to fight on her behalf."

"Marry her? Did she not tell you we are broken off? There is to be no marriage."

"No marriage?" Clarence asked. A crafty look came into his snuff-brown eyes. He had come to see a duel was a thing to be prized. Lords and nabobs—all the go. How Sir Alfred and Mrs. Hering would stare to hear Dammler had called Seville out.

"No, but that is not to say I wish to hear her spoken of with disrespect."

"Certainly not. We can't allow that. Still, it seems to me, Lord Dammler, that as her uncle and guardian, *I* am the one ought to be looking out for her—fighting Seville."

"So you would have done, I'm sure," he lied blandly, "had Seville spoken so to you."

"Yes, yes, that's all well and good, but he spoke of *my* niece. *I* am still her closest male relative. The wedding is off—said so yourself. She is nothing to you now. It is for me to defend her fair name."

"You will be deeply involved, Clarence. My second. It will be your duty to meet with Lord Alvanley and arrange the time and place. He will call on you tomorrow, probably early in the morning."

A call from an out-and-outer like Alvanley was not underestimated. All the go, Alvanley—one heard his witticisms quoted everywhere, still Elmtree did not desire to be second to anyone in defending his niece's name. No actual thought of standing facing an opponent with a gun in his hand at dawn came to mar his visions. It was more the notion of getting rigged out in a black coat and dashing mysteriously through town buying up pistols, having a practice session at Manton's Shooting Gallery, mentioning casually to any noble bystander the purpose of being there that motivated him. "I was obliged to call Seville out—the chap they call The Nabob, you know," had a finer ring to it than "I was Lord Dammler's second." If Dammler wasn't even her fiancé this week, it would sound less fine still. Even there would be an air of cowardice to it, having someone else do his dirty work.

"*I* am her uncle, and I'm your elder too, my boy," he told Dammler, being required to adopt quite a high tone, a new thing for him. He liked it immensely. "You must be ruled by me in this, I think. I will take care of Seville, but you are welcome to be my second."

This was a catastrophe never in his wildest nightmares foreseen by Dammler. Already he knew Prudence would be displeased with the raffishness of a duel fought in her honor. How could he ever face her if, by his mismanagement, it was her uncle that was to be the one firing the shot? What reliance was to be placed on Clarence's doing it with any skill at all?

"There are very strict rules in this matter, Mr. Elmtree," he said, matching his tone to Clarence's. "The etiquette of dueling states that the one to issue the challenge must fight the duel. *I* will fight, and you will be my second, if you agree. Lord Alvanley is Seville's second," he threw in, to show Elmtree that being a second was not below a lord, and therefore not so much below an amateur artist.

"I'll talk it over with Alvanley," Elmtree countered, not quite giving up on his scheme, but disliking to argue about rules and etiquette without a perusal of the rule book.

"He will confirm what I have said," Dammler said at once, then was overcome by a doubt. What if Elmtree, as her closest relative, took precedence? It was too awful to think of. He would override him. He *would not* let Clarence do it.

"We'll be in touch then," Clarence said, and finally, a bottle and many repetitions later, he left, to bound up into his high perch phaeton and go home.

9

Dammler had a dozen times warned Clarence to silence in front of Prudence, but when her uncle smiled on her in the strangest way over their soft boiled eggs, when he castigated Seville (formerly one of his special pets) as a varlet and a scoundrel and predicted he would soon get his comeuppance, her suspicions were alerted. When he then asked her if anyone else had insulted her after Dammler left, she feared the worst.

She already knew there was trouble afoot. To be trundled off home early with Hettie, and to see people staring at her as she left had told her that much. She worried that Dammler had said something horrid about her; once she even got to wondering whether Clarence had ended up in a fight with him, but anything so farfetched as a duel had not crossed her mind. Strangely enough, she had not given a thought to Seville.

"No, Uncle. Did Dammler insult me? What did he say? Why did you go off with him?"

"We had things to arrange. You needn't worry you are disgraced in the least. We don't mean to let the commoner off with it."

"I must know, Uncle! What was said of me? Was there some argument?"

"Argument? Certainly not. That is to say, we had a little argument over which of us is to be the second, but . . ."

"Second what?" she asked, her worst fears far superseded by this telling word.

"It is all rules and etiquette, Prue. I'll look it up at

the library and let you ... No, I can't do that, either. Well, well, never mind. You just run along and write another book, and never fear anyone else will call you a trollop."

"He called me that! Uncle, *who* did such a thing?" Not Dammler. That, at least, was beneath him. She began to have some inkling of the truth at last.

"What can you expect of a foreigner? Don't give it a thought. Dammler and I will call him to account."

Mr. Seville, as English as roast mutton, was a foreigner to Uncle Clarence due to his name that hinted of Spain. "You are having a duel with Seville," she said in a dying voice.

"Nonsense! Where did you get such an idea? If his second calls while I am out, ask him to step in and wait. Lord Alvanley is to come to me. You might show him my pictures while he waits. That will keep him amused. I want to have a look at that rule book. I think *I* am the one ought to be defending you."

"Did *you* call him out?" Oh, but she knew it wasn't that. Dammler and his quick temper had done it. He had always been jealous of Seville. Clarence was to be his second, receiving a call from Seville's second. And fool enough to walk out to the library with such a caller coming!

Conversation with her uncle was never enlightening. She would have to go to Allan to find out what had happened. But first she must insure Clarence's staying home to meet with the second. Her mind was reeling, but it was a good mind, and soon she recalled that a duel might be averted by the proffering and acceptance of an apology. She pleaded with him to accept an apology.

"Widgeon! Seville can't apologize. I know that much. It was Dammler who called him a coward."

"But it was Seville who called me a trollop."

"Worse!" Clarence told her, smiling fondly on her.

"Oh!" She hardly dared ask what.

"That is only a part of it, however. When Seville refused to fight, Dammler called him a coward, and that is what we are going to let on the duel is about, to save your face."

She recognized the hand of Dammler in this face-saving pretext, and realized, too, the inefficacy of it. The truth would soon be bruited about.

"Just what *did* Seville call me?" she asked, steeling herself to hear the worst.

"He is saying he never asked you to marry him at all, the liar, and he sending you all those diamonds."

"Allan said it couldn't be marriage he meant when he sent them. I wonder if he was right."

"Did Seville ask you to marry him or not?"

"I thought he did. I don't know. In my stupidity, perhaps I misunderstood."

She dredged her memory in vain for an actual, outright, unmistakable offer of marriage, and while she recalled mention of a carriage and team of her own, an apartment or house, jewelry, the actual words "Will you marry me," did not come back to her, for they had never been spoken.

"Aye, well he's calling it a carte blanche now, and if that's the way it was, there will be no apologies. Dashed insult, asking a nice girl like you to be his mistress."

"He didn't say anything like that."

"What he meant—told Dammler so."

She could see it all now. Seville, thinking them alienated, had told Dammler the truth. That was the truth then, he had never wanted her to marry him at all. In her naive stupidity she had misunderstood, had told Dammler and a few others. Had remained friends with Seville all these months! And Dammler had known it all along, or suspected. No wonder he had tried repeatedly to turn her against Seville. She was promised to attend Malvern's house party in company with him, too. That must be cancelled. But first there were more urgent matters to attend to. She couldn't think it right to go on urging apology after this insult, and knew Allan would not accept one, in any case. There would be a duel. It must not be Dammler, in no way associated with her now, who fought it.

While they were still talking, Alvanley arrived, and she was told again to run along and write a book, while the men attended to matters. Alvanley was a little surprised to be offered wine and a viewing of a bunch of artworks when he had come to arrange a duel. He was a strict sportsman; had told Seville he must by no means accept an apology for the "coward," or he would be laughed out of the Four Horses Club. This being the case, Seville was not inclined to apologize for his part in the name calling. In the end, there was no mention of any apologies, but only the fixing of the date and place, at seven the next morning, at Hampstead Heath, and the arrangement for a physician.

"Knighton. I always have Knighton," Clarence advised.

Alvanley was hard put to suppress a chuckle. "Knighton does not take part in such affairs as this. Marlowe is our man. I have arranged it."

"Good. Excellent chap, Marlowe. Does he know what he is about?"

"You may be sure he does, Mr. Elmtree. Now, I think that is all."

"Just one little detail. About the second—I think Dammler and I will switch."

105

"That is highly irregular, sir."

"Aye, so it is, but the thing is, they are really fighting over that damned foreigner insulting my niece, and as Dammler isn't going to marry her, after all, I think it is my place to fight."

"They are fighting over Dammler's calling Seville a coward."

"Devil a bit of it. That is only done to try to save the girl's name."

"In that case, sir, the less said of it the better."

"Ho, what's the point of that, with Seville shouting from the rooftops he offered her a mistress-ship?"

"I hadn't realized it was done in quite so public a way as that," Alvanley proclaimed, shocked to find himself on the side of such a dastard.

"To go announcing it at Lord Petersham's ball is as good as putting it in the papers," Clarence informed him.

Alvanley began to suspect Seville had been withholding details from him, and was rather inclined to side with the uncle. "Dammler is not marrying her, you say?"

"No, he has sheered off on her."

"His challenging Seville indicates . . ."

"He never could stand the fellow. No more could I—sending her diamonds."

"I wonder you didn't call him out sooner!"

"So do I. I would have done it, but he kept getting away on me. I would have done it long ago if I could have ever caught up with him."

Never in a long career of arranging such matters as this had Lord Alvanley found himself in just such a pickle. A lady publicly slandered, and being defended by a gentleman who had already called off the wedding. "It seems to me in this circumstance Dammler has behaved irregularly. You are the girl's guardian. If he is not to marry her . . ."

"He has no thought of it. None at all. Well, his behavior has always been a trifle irregular, if it comes to that. Writing verses . . . So you agree with me then that *he* should be the second—Dammler."

"Yes, but in that case it is Dammler I ought to be meeting with this morning."

"Run along and see him. Tell him we have decided he is to be the second."

Alvanley began to think it a very good idea to have a word with young Dammler, and left to do so. They exchanged words for an hour, with Alvanley, the senior gentleman, an acknowledged master on all matters of sportsmanship, laying down the law quite severely. "It is for her guardian to defend her name. He wishes to do so, Dammler, and it will add an unnecessary air of intrigue to the affair for you, no longer involved with the girl, to call him out."

"Damme I've already called him out, and he's accepted."

"You shouldn't have. There is really no excuse your being mixed up in this at all. I have a mind to tell Elmtree to choose a different second."

A vision of Sir Alfred arose in Dammler's mind. Those two babies at the mercy of Seville and Alvanley filled him with horror. "In that case, I'll become her fiancé again. Will that do, sir?"

"Oh certainly, but can it be done?"

"It can, if necessary."

"Highly irregular. How am I to arrange a duel when the principals keep changing place? We'll have to postpone it a day. Make it the day after tomorrow—same time and place. I'll have to see Marlowe *again*. What a

107

nuisance it is. It is what comes of letting parvenus into the Four Horses Club."

"All right. Day after tomorrow. Seven o'clock, you said?"

"Yes, and mind you don't kill your man, Dammler. Damned ramshackle business. A hit in the shoulder will satisfy the lady's honor."

Dammler, as quick to settle down as to wrath, was already half wishing he had been satisfied with drawing Seville's cork, but was not about to admit it. When his caller left, he put on a clean shirt and went around to Grosvenor Square, just as Prudence was setting out for Hettie, whose company she meant to ask for to go with her to Dammler.

"I must speak to you," she said.

He knew then Clarence had told her about it. Foolish to hope he would not. "Come, we'll talk in the carriage," he said, handing her into his closed carriage, driven on this occasion to give him some privacy, as he had discovered he was once again a subject of curiosity to the gawkers.

"Why did you call Seville out?" she began, deeming it wise to take the offensive in an effort to gain the upper hand.

"I called him a coward because he is one."

"No one will believe that story! You're fighting him because he insulted *me*, aren't you?"

"Certainly not."

"Don't treat me like an idiot. Clarence told me everything."

"Why do you waste time asking then?"

"It is not for *you* to take up the cudgels on my behalf. If Selville has been telling anyone he made me an improper offer, it is for my uncle to deal with him. It has nothing to do with you."

108

"I happen to be the one he told! I called him a coward, and I shall fight him. Now there is a little unpleasant business connected with it, Prudence."

"A marvel of understatement."

"One bit more unpleasant than the rest I mean. I have been talking to Alvanley. In order for me to fight this duel, he feels it will be more proper if we resume our engagement, temporarily."

"No! We are a big enough laughingstock already, turning our engagement off and on like a tap. Oh, I'll never dare to show my face on the streets again. I am ruined."

"It is precisely to avoid that possibility that this duel is being fought."

"No, it is being fought because you have an uncontrollable temper! Will it add to my consequence that I have caused a duel? Since when is that considered a feather in anyone's bonnet?"

"It's more of a feather than having Seville tell the world the truth. He never asked you to marry him. Never meant that at all, as I suspected all along. How could you be so *ignorant* as to think he meant anything of the sort?"

"Sorry I couldn't have jauntered off to Cambridge for four or five years to be sly enough to understand the deceit and duplicity of *men!*"

"Oh you're naive to the point of absurdity," he said.

"Maybe I am, but I still don't want you fighting a duel with Seville over me. I want Clarence to do it."

"Prudence, he wouldn't have the chance of a snowball in hell against Seville! He's an expert shot."

"I suppose you are, too?"

"Certainly I am."

"What must be done then is to get Seville to delope. Likely when he sees it is only Clarence standing up against him, he *will* delope. He can have nothing against Uncle, after all."

"Uncle is not standing up against him! *I* am, and as you have caused all this bother, you can damned well be engaged to me for a few more days. You won't look half so foolish as I do, risking my hide for a woman who makes a mockery of me in public."

"Why did you do it then, if you hate me so much?"

"I didn't say I hate you. It is my fault you ever got mixed up with the likes of Seville. I hope I know my duty. I put you in this position, and I shall extricate you."

"What happened *exactly?* What did Seville say?"

"He made some disparaging statements about you—you know the nature of them. There is no point repeating all that unpleasantness."

"I want to know. What did he say?"

"He said he offered you a carte blanche, and you choose to tell everyone he had offered you marriage."

"I didn't tell a soul but you and Hettie, and of course my family."

"He will tell considerably more people his story if he is not stopped."

"Yes, he must be stopped. I see the necessity for that, but you sha'n't be the one to do it. If I have made you look a fool by my book—and I must say no one else takes it so much amiss—then I sha'n't aggravate the offense by having you defend my name."

"No one else was engaged to you."

"Neither were you, at the time you challenged him."

"You never formally cancelled the engagement—there was no notice printed in the papers."

"The date of the wedding came and went. You didn't find me at the church, did you? Mama sent out cards to those invited. For the others, it is none of their busi-

110

ness. Neither is this duel any of yours. Alvanley is quite correct—he is bound to know the proper procedure, and if he says it is up to Clarence, then I shall abide by his decision. We all must."

"Alvanley says if we resume the engagement . . ."

"*If*, but we are not going to!"

"We are!"

She turned on him, furious. "Since when is it possible for a man to become engaged to a woman who has turned him down?"

"It isn't to be a real engagement, if that's what you fear."

"It isn't to be a false one, either. My God, what you were thinking of to call him out! Raking up all that old business again, when it was well forgotten."

"It wasn't forgotten by Seville. It was *he* who raised the point, and I must say I find it hard in you to revile me for doing the proper thing."

"I don't know why men must feel the most troublesome, vexatious, *brutish* course is the proper one. Why didn't you just punch him, if you felt it necessary to defend my tarnished name?"

"I did," he answered, with a certain satisfaction.

"Not at the ball! Not in front of everyone!"

"There weren't many people around, and he hightailed it out pretty fast."

"Oh I think you *like* being the center of attention. You glory in it. Why else would you carry on as you do, going into public with Cybele, setting up that garish apartment with Turkish trappings, and asking those girls to *stroke* you, as though you were an alley cat!"

"No, no, Prudence. I am a dog. You can't have it both ways."

"You probably arranged for me to find you with

111

Cybele so I'd break the engagement and put you in the limelight again. This duel is more of the same."

He stared at her, beyond words, but Dammler was never long speechless. "By the same token, I suppose I chose the most illustrious bride I could find? The exalted, famous Miss Prudence Mallow, cynosure of all eyes!"

"Oh, no. It was *expected* you would choose a gaudy beauty. You got better coverage out of an unknown spinster. A certain shock value attached to Lord Dammler's marrying a nobody."

"You were not unknown!"

"No, not after you got through with me. I'll never be unknown again. Thanks to you I'll go down in history as one of your playthings, a curious footnote in the infamous career of the Marquess of Dammler. Well I'll tell you this, Allan, I don't mean to be remembered as the cause of your untimely demise. If I am in the unenviable position of requiring my honor defended, it isn't you who will do it."

"I have no intention of meeting my end at Seville's hands. I have withstood daggers and arrows, swamp fever and malaria, and it will take more than that damned jackrabbit to finish me off."

"You're not quite immortal. Not a god, impervious to bullets, despite your high opinion of yourself."

"I never said I was. I am not so foolish as to have my head turned by the adulation of the motley mob. I am a fair shot, however."

"If you take a shot at Mr. Seville in my name you had better be immortal."

"What is that supposed to mean?"

Of course, it didn't mean a thing but that she was very cross. "It means I refuse to resume the engagement. Clarence will defend me. He will have the sense

112

to delope, or at least not kill Seville. This must be done as decently as possible. I don't want to be the cause of anyone's death. Oh, how did I get into this predicament?" she wailed.

Reviewing his own case, Dammler felt he was in the worse one. *He* had called Seville out, precipitated a duel that would almost certainly kill her uncle if he didn't arrange it so he could be the principal. He tried once more. "Alvanley says that if . . ."

"Alvanley may go to the devil! You are not fighting Seville. I refuse to have anything to do with any engagement that allows you to murder in cold blood, and do it in my name."

"All right, then. I won't kill him. A hit in the shoulder."

"How do you know he will do the same?"

"I don't."

"That's suicide."

"Call it Spanish roulette. I don't think Seville will shoot to kill."

"He certainly won't shoot to kill Clarence. That is the saner course, to pit Clarence against him."

"It seems to me you take a very cavalier attitude towards poor Clarence."

"Well I like that, and *you* are the one chose him for a second!"

"Yes, a *second*, with no danger attached to the position. Not the principal."

"We are wasting time and words. My mind is made up."

"I am sending in our engagement announcement today."

"If you do, I'll send a retraction in six-inch letters in the next edition."

"I don't mean to go fish-fagging through the columns

113

with you, Prudence. You must allow me to be the judge in this matter."

"I wouldn't allow you to judge a mouse in the matter of morality. Clarence will fight the duel."

Her mind was made up, and when, after a great deal of arguing, he returned her to her door, she hadn't budged an inch, but only become more set in her position. "If I hear of you arranging matters so that you fight Seville, I'll—I'll never speak to you again," were her parting words, and she wished she could have made the threat a good deal stronger.

Considering them as he returned to Berkeley Square, the optimist had soon placed a hopeful construction on the thing. She meant to go on seeing him afterwards then. There were sufficient insults in her talk to provide some anger, too, but over all, it was easy to imagine her concern that he not fight Seville to rest on a fear for his safety. If he stood up with Seville and lived, she would surely not mind. In fact, she would likely have a better opinion of him, whereas if Clarence got himself killed, as was entirely possible, she would really never forgive him. He would never forgive himself. No, certainly he must fight Seville.

He tried his hand at convincing Clarence the engagement was on, but Clarence had already had words with Prudence. He could rearrange anything to his own advantage, but no rearranging was necessary on this occasion. Niece and uncle were as one in wishing the honor of being shot at to be Clarence Elmtree's.

10

The evening preceding the duel was a cool, damp one. Clarence felt twinges of rheumatism in his elbow as he painted Prudence, arrayed in a red-fringed shawl, as became a seductress. He was half in love with her himself, to think of her having got an improper offer from a nabob, a proper one from a marquess, and caused a duel, all before her twenty-sixth birthday. The red carmine was blotched on with an extravagant, loving hand. Nothing was too good for her. As she left the room, he told her to sleep in the morning. No need for her to lose an hour's sleep to see him off. A dasher like Prue had to stay in looks.

"You might have a cup of tea ready against my return," he said casually.

She felt so guilty that she was properly penitent and respectful, and insisted she would be up to see him off. "And home," she added.

"Aye, if I get home," he sighed.

"Uncle, cannot something be arranged with Seville—some word got to him that you mean to delope?" she asked, having a good idea this would break some item of a gentleman's code of honor, but not worrying overly that this would deter Clarence.

"I'm not afraid of him," Clarence assured her. Nor was he. He went to bed and slept like a baby. Even over his tea the next morning he was as merry as a grig, making jokes about this being his last meal. Not till he was in Dammler's carriage with the pistol between his fingers did it occur to him what a lethal thing a gun was. At Manton's Shooting Gallery it had seemed great sport. How some of the gentlemen managed to culp that tiny wafer was a great mystery. He hadn't hit it more than once—could hardly see it in fact. Once he had sneezed and taken a corner out of it.

"What we must do is let Seville know you mean to delope," Dammler said, his chin in his hands, trying to figure a resolution to this awful problem. Lord, and if Clarence *tried* to delope he might well hit Seville in the heart. He had never seen such a poor shot as Clarence. "Aim for the sky," he commanded.

"I'll be shooting high," Clarence replied, distracted. He was looking pale, as the moment of truth approached. "Shall we just let a window down and get a breath of air. It's close in here."

Dammler let down the window, feeling the need of air himself, and Clarence did the same on the other side. The dust from the horses and wheels bothered Dammler, and he had soon rolled his up again, but Clarence's head was hanging out the window. For the first time in the acquaintance of this oddly-matched pair, they were both silent. A duel, Clarence thought! Men standing up and shooting at each other as though they were wafers at Manton's, giant wafers providing a target that even he might hit. It wasn't right to kill anyone. "Thou shalt not kill." It was right in the Commandments. Even in those old days of the Bible when nobody spoke English they knew it was a sin to kill anyone. Yet, it was impossible to back out. He did the hardest philosophizing he had ever done in his life, trying to extricate himself from the morass, but in the end manners seemed more important than morals. He would have to account to Alvanley and society that same day, whereas he might have years to patch it up with the Almighty. He would have to do it. Have to

116

stand up, but he wouldn't shoot to kill, or even injure. A bit of dirt from the carriage flew up and caught him in the eye. He reached to rub it out.

Glancing at him, Dammler thought he was crying, and felt pity for the foolish old man. "Better close the window," he said.

Clarence did so, still rubbing his eye with his other hand. "Got something in my eye," he said, rubbing harder.

"Here, let me get it out," Dammler said, pulling out his handkerchief. Then he was struck with inspiration. Clarence shouldn't shoot with something in his eye. He made some pretense to remove the dirt, while shoving it a little higher under the lid. "I can't seem to get ahold of it," he said.

"It'll work its way out," Clarence said. It was half a relief to be able to shed a tear without Dammler suspecting it was weakness that caused it.

The dirt did not work its way out, and when their carriage reached Hampstead Heath, it was giving some trouble, causing the eye to water copiously. Alvanley had been at great pains to get Seville to delope. As it was known by now, Elmtree couldn't hit the broad side of a barn door, it would be infamous to hit the old man. The whole thing was a fiasco in Alvanley's opinion, and he was sorry he had anything to do with it. Seville had been talked into accepting this role, and was relieved in the extreme that it wasn't that sharpshooter of a Dammler he must stand up against. Fellow would kill him as quick as look at him—had always hated him. He noted with relief that Elmtree was disabled, even thought it was an act, to call the duel off altogether. But no, Alvanley had had enough of putting off, and was not in favor of any postponement. He decreed Dammler should replace Elmtree. It was irregular of

117

course, but when Seville pointed this out, Dammler was only too happy to call him a coward again, and institute a new duel. This removed any quibble of a doubt in the matter. Dammler was so jubilant at the decision that he burst into a smile, a smile that sent Seville's heart sinking. It was all a trick! Dammler was out to kill him!

Clarence, unable even to play the minor roll of charging the pistol, lent the weight of his presence while Alvanley did it, then sat on a tree stump, looking about in the cool morning at the low-lying fog, the bits of dew shining on the grass, the trees shaded into a green mist by the moisture in the air, and thought what a pretty picture it would make. He would try his hand at painting it when he got home, if only this dashed cinder would flow out of his eye. He took another poke at it, and his eye felt better. He batted the lid a few times, realizing the cinder was out. He then directed his full attention to the scene being enacted before him. Dammler and Seville were standing together; they were turning and walking each their twelve paces. What a dandy scene it would make for one of Nevvie's plays. He'd tell him to slip it into his next one. Do it just like this—the foggy morning, the two tall young gentlemen in black, their collars turned up to hide the target of the white triangle of a shirt, Alvanley standing there watching them. Then as he looked, the men stopped walking, turned without either one of them so much as giving a tremble in the arm, and a deafening clap of guns going off was in his ears. Nevvie pointed his gun up high, just as they had decided. Not quite at the sky, more over Seville's shoulder. Flickering his gaze to Seville, he disliked what he saw. The man wasn't aiming at the sky at all. He was aiming

118

right at Nevvie's chest! Then some little look of confusion flashed across Seville's face.

When Seville saw Dammler replace Elmtree, the duel became no longer a farce but a fight to the death. There wasn't one doubt in his mind that Dammler meant to kill him, and his own resolution was equally firm. He aimed for the heart, but in the split second between aiming and pulling the trigger, he noticed Dammler's gun muzzle was up. He lifted his own hand as quickly as possible, in that instant. The bullet was deflected enough to miss the heart. It thudded into Dammler's left shoulder. With mute horror, Seville realized Dammler had deloped. He wasn't touched—the bullet came nowhere near him. He stood silent, shaking and staring, to see if Dammler would topple over.

He did not. The gun fell from his right hand, and he clutched at his shoulder. There was a murderous light in his eyes. He regretted his own generous action, but was too wounded to do anything about it. Alvanley saw the whole, and from experience was pretty sure the wound was not a mortal one. He yelped for Marlowe, who came running forward with his black bag. Dammler was bleeding freely, but not unconscious. He had his jacket stripped away, his shirt torn off, and there in the cool meadow the wound was examined.

"Get him into a carriage," Alvanley ordered.

Seville, all solicitude and apologies, and Elmtree, all confusion, aided him. Marlowe required the amenities of his dispensary. Elmtree hopped in beside him, looking to Alvanley for any further orders.

"This is a bad business. The less said of it the better," was the man's curt remark to the group. Seville felt he had been badly treated, and would likely be held up as a cur after doing what any normal person would have

119

done. The group disbanded, it being agreed they would all say nothing of the morning's work.

Clarence stood by in Marlowe's dispensary watching as the bullet was extracted. While the forceps probed into the gaping wound and Dammler sat grimacing in silent agony, he was happy it was not himself who had stood up to be a target, but once it was out and a bandage was being wrapped around the shoulder, he felt Dammler had been a bit hasty in pushing himself forward to defend Prudence. Wanted to strut around town as a hero, with his arm supported in a sling. "A good thing it's your left arm. It won't interfere with your writing," was his comment.

Dammler said nothing. It had gone as well as he expected. He had saved Elmtree's life and his own. The pain in his shoulder made him nearly unconscious—it was only the brandy that kept his eyes open. "Don't tell Prudence what happened," he said.

"She'll want to know. She'll be waiting there to hear it all. Found out about it somehow."

She had told Dammler she'd never speak to him again if he stood up against Seville, and while the circumstances had not been foreseen, he was still not eager for her to find out. Of course, she would hear sooner or later. There was no chance of Clarence's keeping it quiet for long, but he trusted that she would at least be told the whole story. "Don't tell her anything," he repeated, deciding he would go to her and tell her himself. With a crippled shoulder to ignite her sympathy, she would not be intractable. But first he must get home and have a rest to recoup his strength. Clarence took him to Berkeley Square. Before parting they spoke again of remaining silent on the subject, with Dammler unfortunately using the phrase "gentleman's agreement." Now Clarence was a gentleman, called

120

himself and had often been called one, but to hear the words on the tongue of a lord lent them a new and marvelous significance. It was a different kind of gentleman entirely that included a marquess and a millionaire, and required some different behavior. He resolved to keep the trust. It would be the first time he had ever done so, but it was also the first time he had been involved in such reckless goings-on as a duel. That he was just a little unhappy with his own non-part in the affair helped him to silence as well.

Prudence sat waiting on a bed of thorns for his return. She was prey to the worst imaginings and recriminations. Dammler would have had a better chance of defending himself. She ought not to have insisted it be Clarence who stood up in her defense. She had on top of this her mother's gentle chidings. "What will we do if Clarence is *killed?* Nowhere for us to go. His son will come home and take over the house. Three children—there will be no room for us. We must go back to Kent. I wonder if Ronald Springer is still unattached."

"Don't speak so! Uncle will not be killed. Seville will not *kill* him!" Oh, but what if he did? She was as good as a murderess.

"There is no saying with that sort of people. I'm sorry we ever got mixed up with them. This is all Dammler's doings. It was he who introduced you to that Seville."

The morning dragged on for hours while the duel took place, the wound was dressed and the victim got home. When at last Clarence returned to Grosvenor Square, the ladies had reached a state bordering on distraction. What a blessed sight to see him walking up to the door. Not dead, not wounded, not anything but dear old Uncle Clarence, looking sobered by his ordeal, but alive. Prudence dashed to him and threw herself

121

crying on his neck. "Oh, Uncle, I'm sorry! I'm sorry! Can you ever forgive me?" she sobbed.

He was bathed in forgiveness and pride at his recklessness at nearly participating in a duel. "Now, now, what is this? Tears? I thought you would have a pot of tea ready against my victorious return," he smiled benignly.

"How about Mr. Seville? Is he—is he alive?" she asked fearfully.

"Yes, yes, I didn't kill him," Clarence told her.

"I am so happy you both deloped," she said.

She was not allowed off with this misapprehension. "Deloped! No such a thing! *He* did not delope. Aimed right for the heart, the scoundrel, but he is a wretched shot."

"He has the reputation of being an **excellent** shot," she reminded him.

"He won't have after today's work," Clarence said, but then he said no more, so Prudence was free to believe. Clarence was touching up the picture to suit himself. It was fatally easy to imagine both men had deloped, and Clarence was adding to his glory by pretending, or even by now believing, Seville had aimed to kill.

Between his own ignominious part in the duel and his "word of a gentleman," Clarence kept a tight check on his tongue. He grew into a perfect model of taciturnity as the day progressed. Prudence concluded she was in the doghouse because of losing her lord, and kept pretty well out of his way. Her mama was of the same mind and behavior, so it was necessary for him to seek them out to be silent before them, to stand looking stern and noble, which expression bore such a strong resemblance to his more customary sulks that it was mistaken for that.

122

"Where is Lord Dammler?" Prudence once ventured to inquire, which brought her a rather testy reply.

"Gone home to bed."

"To *bed?*" she asked, incredulous.

Seeing he had skated dangerously close to letting the cat out of the bag, Clarence rushed on to conceal it. "Was up half the night carousing, and had his eyes half closed all through the duel. He has gone home for a rest. I daresay you'll see him later."

Dammler lay in his bed waiting for Prudence to come to him. She would know by now, he thought at mid-afternoon. He made no effort to bring himself to a healthier appearance. He lay pale and weak against the pillows, with the blood seeping through his bandages, spurning food and drink that he might look as pitiful as possible when she came. She would not be so hardhearted as to hold it against him he had done what he had. Who had suffered but himself? Why had he done it but for her? Impossible she should be anything but grateful. The romance and drama of it must appeal to her heart, even if her head pretended to be displeased. But why didn't she come? When still he lay alone at nightfall, he saw he had miscalculated the affair in some manner. Certainly she would have had the whole story long since from Clarence. Was she such a monster she felt no remorse for her part in it? Was she really angry with him—so angry she didn't intend to come to see how he went on? He might be dying for all she knew! He could not eat, but he drank a little wine and fell into a state that was half coma, half sleep.

By morning, it was more than half coma, and accompanied by a fever as well, so that his servants sent off for Lady Melvine. Hettie was soon bustling into his room, bursting with curiosity. She looked with acute dismay at the unmoving body in the bed, felt his forehead, and sent a footman off for Dr. Knighton. Knighton came and undid the bandage to find a wound, infected, with angry red streaks beginning to run into the shoulder and down along the arm. He prophesied a bad spell, possibly worse fever and delirium, both of which came true. Hettie sat by his bed till he was conscious, urged broth and liquids on him, quizzed him as much as his condition allowed, till she had got the gist of the story from him.

"What of Prudence? Why does she not come?" she asked, perplexed.

"She's mad that I took Clarence's place, I expect."

"She has some gall, being mad at anything! She ought to be here on her knees, apologizing. I have a good idea to go over there and give her a piece of my mind."

"No! If she doesn't come of her own accord, we'll let her alone."

At Grosvenor Square, Prudence sat in a similar state of perplexity and offense that Dammler did not come to her. The duel, she assumed, had gone off in a satisfactory manner. Clarence was alive and well; Seville, too, had survived. Was it not odd he didn't come and speak to them about it? The whole affair was *his* doing—*he* had called Seville out. He cared enough for her reputation that he had done that, so why did he not come? She questioned Clarence discreetly as to Dammler's attitude on the fateful morning. Had he been angry?

"Not a bit of it. He was cool as a cucumber."

"Do you not think you ought to call on him, Uncle?"

"What for? He knows where I am if he wants to stop around."

Clarence knew Nevvie would not stop around till he got his arm out of the sling—a day or two. There was enough of shame in his own part that he was reluctant

124

to call, but after a few urgings by Prudence he did stop by one afternoon three days after the duel, when he figured the sling would be abandoned, and he might bring Dammler home with him.

He found Dammler recovering, but pretty close to being hostile. "Not scribbling?" Clarence asked merrily. "I made sure you would be dashing off the whole into a play. You must do it. It would make a dandy dramatic scene, and there would be no need to use real bullets, of course."

"I don't write farce, Mr. Elmtree. How is Prudence? What does she think of the affair?"

"She has asked me a dozen times why I don't call on you, and that is why I am here. She wants to know how you go on."

This conveyed to Dammler that Prudence knew he was wounded. "Be sure to tell her I am fine."

"I certainly will. She will be happy to hear it. She has been worried sick about you."

"Not worried enough to call in person, however."

"You know how busy she keeps herself. Shall I tell her you want to see her?"

"No! No, thank you," he said angrily.

"She wouldn't begrudge the time in the least."

"Very generous of her, but I wouldn't like to tear her away from more worthwhile pursuits."

This cool reception of Prue's inquiries threw Clarence into a dudgeon. He told his niece he had gone to see the poet, and he was as toplofty as a lord.

"Did he ask for me?" she inquired quite shamelessly, for she was becoming desperate for news.

"He mentioned how you were taking it. I said as well as could be expected."

"He didn't say he would call?"

"No, no, he won't be calling," Clarence said gruffly.

He felt uneasy at the duplicity, but bucked up by the specific injunction that it was a great secret, he gave no reason for the lack of calling.

"Is he angry?" she pressed on.

"He is in a bit of a pucker about something," Clarence admitted. "Acting very strange and standoffish. He wasn't like himself at all. Why, I wasn't even offered a glass of wine, now I think of it. I daresay now he has had time to think the business over he is unhappy he ever got drawn into it."

"He pitched himself into it!"

"So he did. It is all his own fault, entirely. Well, we sha'n't bother our minds about Lord Dammler. Isn't it time you got sending another book off to Murray? What is everyone to read it you don't write them a book?"

How was it possible to write under this cloud? She was worried half to death. Not a visit, nor even a note from Allan. He was done with her. She had forgiven him Cybele, but he had not been able to forgive her the book. Never once did it occur to her he was unwell. She did not go out for several days, nor did any of their mutual friends come to call. Hettie had taken the resolve never to speak to the hussy again, and was holding firm to it.

11

Dammler was slow to recover. The spreading poison in his arm weakened him, nor had he any emotional desire to get well quickly. For what? To face a life of disillusionment? He had feigned it in his first youthful cantos, but it had been a joyous cynicism, a good-natured wink at convention with a laugh at the hypocrisy of his own sort of people. This is what we say, and this is what we really do, he had pointed out, with lavish examples, whose very enthusiasm belied any condemnation. He was now feeling condemnatory, the very worst possible frame of mind to promote a cure. But with a hardy constitution and the nursing of Knighton and Hettie, he gradually returned to health. Nor was he allowed to sequester himself in his study and put down on paper all his black thoughts.

"What you want is a new flirt to cheer you up," Hettie told him, her mind already having settled on the very girl, one of the performers in his *Shilla*. She mentioned her choice, and he frowned.

"When I am ready to take up with women again, it won't be an actress," he said. "One day I must find a suitable lady and settle down. Till that time, I mean to do some serious writing."

"Excellent! A new play, Allan. Something bright and lively to pull you out of the megrims."

"It was something in the nature of philosophy I had in mind. Possibly a translation of some Latin till I feel more creative."

"Oh, my dear, don't think of it! Enough to lay a

127

healthy man low, and who on earth would be interested to read it?"

Having very little enthusiasm for this project, he did not forge ahead with it, but Hettie proceeded with his cure. If it was marriage that would joggle his mind out of this despond he was settling into, she would find him a bride.

It was not a particularly felicitous season for debs. Really no one she could welcome with open arms as a niece-in-law, but she could do better than Miss Mallow, at least. The Duke of Wykombe had a presentable daughter. A silly little ninny, pretty and eligible. Lady Dorothy was brought to meet him, out of his bed now, and often to be found in his study, surrounded by a depressing wall of books that must be enough to cast the healthiest mind into the dumps. Nor did that empty chair to match Madame du Barry's desk help in the least! The meeting was a disaster. What must Dammler take into his head to discuss that afternoon but physics! He was working out a theory that climate modified behavior, with heat the culprit in the story, from what Hettie could figure.

"Do you mean then that cold is at the bottom of morality?" Lady Dorothy asked, in forgivable confusion.

"There is no such a thing as cold," he told her. "There is only a relative absence of heat."

Lady Dorothy accepted this dictum without argument. "Did you find people more moral in cooler climates?" she asked politely.

"I found them less degenerate," he replied, realizing as he spoke that he preferred the warmer climes, for both bodily temperature and social mingling. He was tainted, a degenerate. He would move north.

"Less comfortable too I should think," Hettie threw in, yawning. "What we ought all to do is board up our fireplaces and put off our wraps and be chilled into goodness. But if there is no such a thing as cold, then there is no point in chasing after it, I suppose."

"It is a relative word—when we say cold, we mean usually less warm than our own body temperature. Though, of course, being relative, it may refer to something other than the human body."

"Tell me, wise philosopher, is there such a thing as foolishness? I must own that relative to your former conversation, I find this discussion without sense," his aunt teased him.

"Folly can be absolute," he decided instantly.

"I give you no argument on that pronouncement. I have the evidence of it before my eyes. Come, Lady Dorothy, let us go before we take a chill in all this lack of heat. Dammler has begun his reformation by putting out his fires."

She gathered up her protegée and took her home. For two days she left Dammler to his own lugubrious thoughts. He wrote three chapters of a horror story, then gave up on his reformation and lit a fire with them.

After two days Hettie hit on the notion of introducing to Dammler a lady of blue reputation, an intellectual who might argue him into spirits. Miss Samson had little looks and no excess of breeding, but she was reputed to be very clever. Hettie raised the matter of physics, telling Miss Samson that Dammler had decreed there was no such a thing as coldness. For three-quarters of an hour she sat back and listened to them go to it. Dictionaries were drawn out to support Miss Samson's theory, while the physics tomes counterattacked with their definition. Poetry and novels were applied to. Left out in the cold, for instance, used the word as a noun, therefore it must exist. Nonsense, that had nothing to do with temperature; it was used figuratively to denote rejection. It was an abstract idea merely.

Was it not possible for one to catch a cold then? An *obvious* colloquialism—and more often accompanied by a fever than a lowering of temperature, thus indicating to the meanest capacity it had nothing to do with the matter under discussion. Miss Samson was ready to argue the point forever, long after Dammler was bored to tears with it. When next Hettie returned, she was commanded never to bring that demmed argumentative female near him again. She had given him a migraine.

"You are too much alone these days, Allan. Time to give a party. Have a housewarming party. I'll look after all the details for you."

"I've already had a housewarming party, the night *Shilla* opened." His glance to Madame du Barry's desk told his aunt what he was thinking.

"I met Miss Mallow on Bond Street the other day," she mentioned casually.

"What a treat for you," he said in a sardonic voice. "And did Miss Mallow deign to inquire how we go on?"

"I didn't give her the chance. I cut her dead. No, don't glare, gudgeon! I didn't make an issue of it. Merely I stopped to look in a window and admire an extremely ugly bonnet when I saw her approach. *She* knew what I was about, but no one watching would have been able to say I snubbed her."

This was acceptable to Dammler. Not one inch out of his way would he go to conciliate her. She was all in the wrong, and she would be the one to give in. He wouldn't even ask Hettie how she looked, and Hettie, her heart hardened against the girl, would not tell him she looked miserable. It occurred to him about this time, however, that he might see her on Bond Street himself with no loss of dignity, and to this end he began to go on the strut at the hour when females were likely to be seen perusing the shops. He haunted the bookstores and libraries, deeming them the likeliest spots to attract her, but saw instead copies of her novel, sitting on the shelves, laughing at him.

Once he met Clarence and nodded to him. This was sufficient encouragement for Elmtree, who was finding life dull without his former great friends to visit, to draw up for a chat. "I see the arm is all better. Glad to see it. What a day it was when we had that little duel, eh, Dammler? I often think of it—but keep it mum, of course!"

"It was a day best forgotten."

"I should say so. I have put it out of my mind long ago. I am very busy with my painting. I am still working in the old style—Rembrandt. I am looking about for a model. You wouldn't know of anyone who would like to pose for me?"

"What sort of person do you mean?"

"I was thinking of that little filly that is in your play. The one that Exxon has got tucked away in a corner. His cousin, I believe. Cybele someone told me her name is."

Dammler found to his surprise that it was still possible to smile. The image of Clarence turning Cybele into one of his mud-brown hags was too ludicrous to consider without a smile. How he would love to see such a picture! But Clarence worked in his home, and to be sending the likes of Cybele there was impossible. "She ain't his cousin, Clarence," he said, laughing, and using the first name against all his best intentions of being standoffish.

"Eh? Lives with him—must be some relation."

"She doesn't quite share his ancestral roof. His wife wouldn't like it. She is his mistress, they tell me at

Drury Lane. Exxon picked her up the very night *Shilla* opened."

Clarence's jaw fell open. "Exxon is not an artist! What does he mean, setting up a mistress?"

"He means to cut us out, I guess. You artists aren't the only gents up to such tricks. In any case you could not well have Cybele to Grosvenor Square to paint her. Not the thing."

"Very true, Wilma would take it amiss. She is very straight-minded about such carryings on. Where did Rembrandt paint his mistress, I wonder."

"I don't know about Rembrandt, but the fellows nowadays have a studio discrete from their homes, where they do the deed. If it is such a highflyer as Cybele you have in your eye, you'd better open up an atelier."

"Eh?"

"A studio, I mean." He said it as something to say, with no thought Clarence would actually do it. Nor did Clarence's own thoughts head in this direction as yet. He only shook his head sadly.

"I am surprised at Exxon," was his comment. A sad comment, though he knew no more of the man than that he was old, and a lord.

"Yes, and *I* am surprised at Cybele." Cybele was but an excuse to prolong the conversation, to work it around to other women. "How is your sister?" he asked, determined not to inquire after the niece.

"She is bored to flinders. She says she won't pose for another picture till after the new year."

"Is there no one else who might pose for you?" he asked, as well as bringing the conversation to Prudence without mentioning her name.

"Sir Alfred promised to make up one of a group for a large painting, but I'm not sure I will tackle 'The

132

Night Watch'—it is a great unwieldy thing, when all's said and done."

"You always excelled at painting women. Young women," Dammler forged on, still withholding the name.

"Aye, I do have a certain knack for a young girl, but if she is his mistress I can't ask her home. Well, I'm off, Dammler. Glad to see you're all better. Prudence will be glad to hear it."

Then he was gone, just as the talk got around to the one subject of interest to Dammler. He recalled the conversation to find hidden traces relating to Prudence in it, with very poor success. She was still at Grosvenor Square—that's all he knew for sure.

Clarence too thought of their talk; he seldom thought of anything else for two days. He must set up a studio—an atelier. How had he not done so, all these years? What interesting specimens he might paint, if he didn't have to choose people that might come into his own home. Derelicts—drunken creatures for instance were dandy subjects, and fallen women. There was nothing so interesting to paint as a woman with a shade of sin about her. Rembrandt, Rubens, all the chaps painted harlots. Why, way back in the days of the Bible wasn't Mary Magdalene herself a prime subject? It was his duty as an artist to record on canvas for posterity the flush of today's harlotry. Posterity would take the notion there wasn't a fallen woman in the country but Emma Hamilton, made to look like a little doll by Romney, if he didn't attend to it.

Without further ado, and without a word to Wilma or Prudence, he went to a real estate agent's office and hired an upper-story room on Bond Street, not far south of Oxford. The ladies saw without protesting that all his painting paraphernalia was being toted away,

133

and soon learned from Sir Alfred what Clarence was up to. They were delighted. No more standing with a broom or mop in the hands for hours at a stretch. No more having to admire his brown blotches. No more lectures on chiaroscuro. It was a blessed relief.

When the atelier was ready for use, Clarence began to look about for a suitable model. Who he really wanted was Cybele, but she was taken, so he must find a substitute. If a man was after a looker, Dammler was the chap to see, and before many hours he was sitting in the saloon on Berkeley Square, waiting for Dammler to come to him.

Dammler's spirits soared to hear Elmtree was waiting for him. It was a rapprochement. He would be invited to Grosvenor Square for dinner. He hastily considered whether he ought to give in and go, when still Prudence had made no personal overture. Perhaps there would be a letter. He was smiling in anticipation when he entered the saloon.

"Mr. Elmtree—Clarence, how kind of you to come," he said, extending his hand. He would relent.

"Not at all. We people in the arts, the creative few, ought to keep in touch. In fact, it is on the subject of art that I am come," he said, dispersing hope in Dammler's breast. He had forgotten all about the idea of a studio, but the conversation turned to it now.

"Yes, you recall you suggested that I ought to set up a discreet little studio, and I have done it, just as you advised."

"I didn't advise you to! I only mentioned others . . ."

"Just so. I ain't slow to take a hint. I have got a discreet little room on Bond and put my things in it. What I want now is a model, and I want you to recommend one for me. One of your ladies, what?" he laughed roguishly.

134

"I don't have any ladies!" Dammler answered, chagrined, and wondering if the old fool had been telling Prudence some story that he had.

"Eh? What about Cybele? I mean to say, you must have replaced her."

"No! No, I didn't! I am not in the petticoat line at all these days, Clarence," he said earnestly.

"What of the fillies in your play? Surely one of them would be happy to pick up a few pounds posing for me."

"You want me to find a professional model for you? Is that what you mean?"

"Exactly. A looker is what I want. A good looking young girl—any of your harem girls will do."

"Oh but they are actresses. They don't pose for artists."

"They don't act in the daytime."

"It is just a *model* you want, Clarence? You aren't thinking of—of anything else?" he asked carefully.

"Oh ho, I see what you are up to, rascal! As to that, *che sera sera,* as the dagoes say. But it is a model I want, right enough," he added as he saw the frown on his host's face. "Can you recommend someone?"

"I am not in the business of whoremongering."

"Had Cybele right in your rooms at Albany."

"Yes, and I had a cheese in my pantry, but I am not a cheese merchant! I might provide you a model, *not* a mistress. I want that perfectly clear."

Clarence saw no distinction. What he wanted was a woman of the sort who wouldn't balk at posing without necessarily all her clothes on. What was the point in painting a harlot if you didn't show a spot of shoulder or ankle, or even the beginning of a breast? How was posterity to know she was a fallen woman and not a wife? "Exactly!" he said.

"I'll ask if any of the girls are interested in posing. Will you have a chaperone present?"

"What for?"

"For propriety's sake."

"There will be gawkers in and out all the time. The studio will be full of people. Sir Alfred makes himself quite at home there, and I hope you will too."

This sounded public enough to satisfy Dammler the model would be subjected to no worse than having a very poor likeness taken. It also opened up a possible avenue of bumping into Prudence, and he agreed. "I imagine your family are anxious to get a look at the studio."

"They are burning with curiosity, both of them. But I didn't let them help me, or they'd be hanging curtains and wanting to put cushions on the chairs. I might as well warn you, the place is not stylish at all. Have you found the ateliers in other countries to be stylish?" he asked, not quite sure he had done right to make the place as austere as possible.

"I generally found the more serious the artist, the less note he took of his surroundings."

This suited Clarence right down to the ground. He was glad he hadn't succumbed to the temptation to have the chairs painted. Lovely, rackety things they were.

The next afternoon Dammler offered the job to one of the worldly creatures at Drury Lane, who could well handle a Clarence Elmtree, and the deal was set. He got in touch with Elmtree at the studio, and agreed to bring the girl himself to show her the route and make the introduction. Both were satisfied with the arrangement.

12

Prudence had thought it was Clarence's presence that hindered her own work. Since he had abandoned Leonardo for Rembrandt, his customers had fallen off. Mrs. Hering, for instance, was not at all eager to pose any longer. When her mother was not doing it, the job fell to herself. With Clarence away for the better part of the day, she would get busy and finish up her latest work. But inspiration was lacking. She sat for hours at a stretch looking at the walls, the paper, the mirror, where she saw a sorrowful face, turning paler by the day. She should get out and take some air.

She went abovestairs to get her bonnet and pelisse. She wore a bonnet chosen for her by Dammler when they were hardly more than acquaintances. It was the prettiest one she owned, and had been insanely expensive, bought at Mademoiselle Fancot's shop. She remembered well the day they had gone together to buy it, and she had, for the first and last time in her life, chosen two bonnets in one day. It had lost its luster. A pretty black affair with a red rose tipping over the brim, but the rose was becoming frayed at the edges. It no longer made her look distinguished, yet it was her best bonnet. New gowns she had got for her trousseau; the bonnets were still to be purchased, due to a lack of funds. She ought to buy a new one. That's what she would do. Go down to Mademoiselle Fancot and buy a new, fabulously expensive chapeau to cheer her up. Maybe she would even see Dammler while she was out.

She'd take a stroll along Bond Street, wearing the new hat.

In the studio, Dammler observed that Sir Alfred was sitting in the watcher's seat with a cigar in his hand, waiting impatiently for the female to arrive. The paints were out, the brushes ready, Elmtree in his smock with a copy of Rembrandt's ugly Saskia as Flora propped up before him, the real model if the truth were allowed to be stated.

While Dammler was noticing that Saskia looked about eight months pregnant in the likeness, Clarence outlined his preparations. "I brought this silk curtain from the guest room to use as a gown. Of course it isn't a gown, but I have this runner to pull around the waist to hold it on, and I can get the sheen of the material well enough from the curtain. It will need a nice impasto to give the luster. I picked up this necklace at the Pantheon—glass beads, but it will give the effect I want. I have my walking stick here with flowers wrapped around it for her to hold, and I'll get the actual big bouquet for her hand later, when I get down to the hands. Today I mean to do the head." He glanced at the picture of Saskia.

"Odd, she is wearing an ostrich plume on her head. She is supposed to be Flora. That means flower, does it not, Dammler?"

"Yes, I think that is a bit of vine around her head, with one frond sticking up," he explained.

"Looks for the world like an ostrich plume to me."

The model arrived and was sent behind a screen to drape herself in the dusty silk curtain, and hang about her throat the glass beads. She was a vivacious woman, currently wearing the jet black tresses that distinguished the cast of *Shilla*. She was a trifle thin-faced, bearing not the slightest resemblance to Saskia's fair complexion and fullness of figure. All this lack of likeness was nothing to Clarence. She would do admirably, except that she required a weed for her hair, a weed that looked like an ostrich plume. None of his own weeds would do the trick. It must stick up, and bend just so over the head, like Saskia's. Weed after weed was put in her hair, only to tumble over her eyes in the most obstinate manner.

"What we'll do is get an ostrich feather and paint it into a fern," Clarence decided.

"Bring one with you next day," Dammler suggested, "and go ahead with the head itself today."

"I start at the top," Clarence told him. "The weed is at the top."

"For this once, could you not . . ."

"I don't tell you how to rhyme up your verses—I daresay you don't begin in the middle of a line—and you may count on it I know a little more about art than yourself. I can't begin without an ostrich feather. We'll have to go out and buy one."

"We" soon became "you," however. While Clarence mixed up his greens, Dammler was to take Miss Penny out to a milliner's and hold ostrich feathers on her head till one drooped just so, bending over the crown of the head without touching the hair, then the painting could proceed.

Shaking his head at the foolishness of it, but with really nothing better to do, Dammler gave in. Miss Penny put off the curtain and he led her down Bond to Conduit Street, to his favorite milliner, Mademoiselle Fancot. Together they tried on feather after feather, finding none that would quite do. The blue hung at just the right tilt, but it was blue. The green was the right shade, but too short, another too long. The proprietress herself, an old business acquaintance of his lordship, entered into the spirit of the thing. There were merry laughs echoing through the shop, audible even behind the curtain, where Miss Mallow sat with three confections before her, choosing first one, then another. She thought it sounded very like Allan, but knew she was imagining him in every shadow, and chided herself for her nonsense. That Mademoiselle Fancot stayed with the company told her the party was no ordinary one, but of the highest *ton*. She herself was completely abandoned. For five minutes she sat, waiting for mademoiselle to come and help her make up her mind. In the end, pushing the three bonnets away, she decided to take her patronage elsewhere, if this was how she was to be treated. She had received better attention when she had first come with Allan! She looked about for her bonnet, then remembered having left it out in the shop. The laughter, she noticed, had subsided.

She came out from behind the curtain of the private room to find Lord Dammler standing with her black bonnet in his hands, looking at it with the strangest expression on his face, half sad, half smiling. The unexpectedness of it, the shock, sent her heart fluttering. He must know it was her bonnet—he had seen it often enough. The look he wore suggested the bonnet had aroused memories, fond memories, surely, of those past days. The tender expression suggested it. She wondered at his being here, and assumed, after a quick glance around the shop, that he had seen her enter, and come in after her. There were a few other patrons about, but none of them being paid any heed by him. There was also one gentleman—the laugher, no doubt.

When he looked up and saw her, he said, "Prudence!" in quite a startled voice, that would have told her he had no notion she was there, had she not been too shaken to think of it.

She smiled nervously and reached out for her hat. "I see you have designs on this bonnet, Dammler, but I must caution you it is already taken. It is mine."

"Good Lord! So that's how it came to be here! I recognized it. You have often worn it in the past."

"Yes, often enough that I had plans to retire it, but can find none I like better." And still he held on to it, though her hands had been outstretched for a long minute. "Well, are you going to steal it from me?" she laughed, quickly concluding he was as ill at ease as herself.

"Sorry." He gave it over to her, and stood looking as she peeped into the mirror to put it on. He stayed at her elbow, watching her perform this feminine chore. When she had it on, he reached out to tilt it at a little more rakish angle than she usually wore. It was hardly the act of an inveterate enemy.

Each looked at the other with a conscious eye, wondering what to say, and what to do. It seemed too good an opportunity to let slip away. Dammler had sworn a dozen times he would make no move towards reconciliation, but with no move having been made on her part over a period of a few weeks now, and with so few chances to meet her, he was losing all his patience. He was also aware that Miss Penny lurked in the corner with Mademoiselle, wishing to grab his attention. One did not present an actress to a lady, and he assumed both Miss Penny and Mademoiselle Fancot were aware of it, and would bear with him a moment.

"Well, and how do you go on, Prudence?" he asked, striking a compromise between what he wished to say and what he had sworn he would not.

"You have stolen my line," she answered with a laugh, prey to much the same feelings as himself.

"Again," he added. "I refer obliquely to plagiarism, if that remark seems inappropriate."

"It will hardly do you credit. Not one of my brighter epigrams. But to answer your question, I am fine, thank you. And yourself?"

"Fine."

"He steals my answer, too. My bonnet, my question, my answer. I had better have an eye to my change purse, or he'll be relieving me of my shillings and pence."

"You will require all you possess, if you mean to shop here. Shockingly expensive."

"I know it well. I am throwing caution to the winds to venture in here. You have led me into these expensive habits. It was you who introduced me to the establishment."

Dammler was bereft of a clever answer. He had been away from her too long. His wits had become rusty, and to add to his *gêne,* there stood Miss Penny, casting questioning glances on him. Still he wished to stay with Prudence, prolong the casual meeting. "What are you writing these days?" he asked.

"You wish to steal my plots and characters, too, I suppose, but I still carry on with *Patience.* Truth to tell, I become impatient with the girl. What are you doing?"

"Oh—this and that. A few translations, nothing of much interest."

"Ah, well, if it is *translations* you are into, show off, my opinion would be of no use to you. I am quick enough to criticize Lord Dammler, but if it is Homer or one of those lofty gents you are tackling, I leave your fate to the reviewers."

This sounded marvelously encouraging. As good as an offer to call. How should she give her opinion on

142

what he was doing if he didn't bring it for her to see? He quickly invented some work that would make a visit plausible. "I have started a novel," he said, then remembered he had also finished the novel at the end of Chapter Two by burning it. He'd scribble it up again.

"Indeed! How interesting! What is it about?"

Her eager friendliness dissolved any last traces of being standoffish. "Why don't I give you a drive home and we can discuss it? I have my chaise right around the corner." Oh, Lord—how was he to get it here from the studio? And what was he to do with Miss Penny? "Or do you have a carriage waiting?" he asked, in some little doubt and confusion.

"No, I came in a hired cab. Uncle, you must know, has set up a studio off the premises and keeps his carriage away all day. I am bursting with curiosity to have a look at the studio."

"Have you not seen the atelier? I have been there several times."

"He didn't say so!" she answered, surprised.

There were a million things she wanted to say to him, and the feeling was mutual. With a worried glance over his shoulder to Miss Penny, he tried to think of some way of getting out without letting on he was with her. But Miss Penny, overhearing that he was offering to take the lady home, came towards him.

"I hope you don't plan to leave me here alone!" she said in an injured voice.

Prudence looked at the girl and felt a perfect fool. Dammler had come here with that woman! It was what she should have expected. The girl was a high flyer, pretty, a shade vulgar. And here she had thought he followed herself into the shop. The laughing and talking—it was him with this woman! All his little bits of constraint were clear to her now. He had been wanting to be rid of her the whole time. Watching her, Dammler read her every thought.

"Prudence, it's not what you think," he said, taking her by the elbow and leading her quickly to the door. "She is an actress from *Shilla*. I only brought her here to buy a feather."

"Only a feather! You are become clutch-fisted in your old age. You used to buy them the whole bonnet, and a gown to go with it."

"The girl is nothing to me. I scarcely know her. I'll send her off in a cab. Wait!" He turned to speak to Miss Penny.

Prudence could not trust herself to speak. She left quickly without another word, but a look that expressed all her disgust with him.

13

The incident provided just the incentive Prudence
needed to jostle her out of her lethargy. No point
thinking if she sat around waiting long enough Dammler
would come back. He was into his old habits of carrying
on with the lightskirts, straight on the road to hell, and
it was the right road for him. Her new friends had
fallen off with a sudden rush after the duel. She didn't
know whether Dammler himself had a hand in it, but
in any case Hettie was cutting her dead, and Hettie
wielded considerable influence in society. No matter,
there was more than one society in London. In the
literary circles her credentials were still untarnished.
She invited a few of the lesser luminaries in her own
sphere to a social evening at Grosvenor Square. Miss
Burney, the well-known novelist, sent in her regrets,
but others came and soon a few invitations were being
received to genteel do's. She did not precisely enjoy
them, but they helped to get by the long days and
interminable evenings.

Dammler, she assumed, had given up literature entirely, for there was never a sign of him. Even at a small,
select dinner given by Mr. Moore for quite the cream of
writers, he was not present, and he was known to be a
particular friend of Thomas Moore. His name did arise,
however, when Leigh Hunt inquired if anyone had
heard of him recently.

"Hunt wants to borrow money," Moore warned her
aside. "Always putting the bite on his friends. Keep your
reticule closed, Miss Mallow, or he'll be hitting you up

for a loan." Then Moore turned to the group and said he had heard Dammler was doing some translations.

"He is also working on a novel," Prudence added.

"Humbug!" Mr. Rogers laughed. "Dammler ain't writing at all nowadays. He has taken up painting, instead."

"Really! Well, he always was interested in art," Moore mentioned.

"More interested in the models," Rogers pointed out with a knowing look. "He is to be found two afternoons out of three at Bond Street, where a new artist has set up his shop."

Prudence listened, trying to suppress her gasps of astonishment. They could not mean Clarence's studio! Yet Dammler had mentioned being there, and it was on Bond Street. And hadn't Uncle been acting very sly lately? Wearing Belcher kerchiefs for one thing, but she had thought he was only aping the artistic school. Was it possible Clarence was painting young women of shady reputations? What else could account for Dammler's being there?

"Whose shop is that?" one of the throng asked.

"Fellow name of Oaktree, something of the sort," Rogers replied.

"Was it, by any chance, Elmtree?" Prudence asked, trembling inside.

"That's it! Fellow's a regular block in any case. It struck me he was well named. Churns out portraits as if they were sausages—cooked sausages. He uses a deal of brown. Yes, it was quite a pretty little sausage he was dabbing up on canvas t'other day I stopped by. An actress from Drury Lane. Dammler's flirt, I believe. He was there dancing attendance, in any case."

At this point it was recalled by Mr. Moore that the young lady at his left had an historical interest in Lord Dammler, and he adroitly steered the conversation aside. It chanced to be a subject that also interested the lady greatly. "I am going to Finefields for a house party," he mentioned to the group. "Lady Malvern is having a literary gathering next week. You go, I think, Mr. Rogers?"

"I go, but I have warned Malvern I will take my paper and books with me and excuse myself from the duty of making up to his wife. I fancy she'll ask Dammler along, as the rest of the party is such dull dogs as you and I, Tom," he said in a joking way to Moore.

Mr. Moore was having uphill work getting off the topic of Lord Dammler. In desperation, he turned to Prudence. "Have you been to Finefields, Miss Mallow?"

"No, I was invited earlier this year, actually, but was unable to attend."

"You should come along next week. You will find the company to your liking, I think."

"Yes," she answered, a little wistfully. But how was it possible to go without an invitation? She was the last person in the world to be asked, when she had specifically told Constance she disliked being in company with writers. Such a foolish thing to have said, but it was only a jibe at Allan.

The conversation that evening was bright. These men and women possessed some of the keenest minds and liveliest wits in London, but they might as well have discussed the weather for all the attention Prudence paid to them. What was going on in Clarence's studio? Had Dammler led Clarence into leading the sort of life he led himself? It sounded strangely like it, yet Clarence was generally to be found at home in the evenings, or his absence accounted for by some innocent diversion. She must get down to that studio.

She tackled Clarence on the subject the next morning over breakfast. So involved as she had been in her own life, she had hardly observed the gradual change in his appearance, but as she scrutinized him across the breakfast table, she observed he had been metamorphosed into a poor caricature of an artist. He had let his hair grow down past his ears. It was not brushed sedately back as he used to wear it, but floated wildly about him in a henna halo. He had tinted his hair before—the shade was not entirely new, perhaps brighter. Around his neck rested not a white cravat but a gaudy scarf in blue and green. His shirt was open at the neck, and a small golden chain hung there, partially concealed by the scarf. The chain she felt was a recent enough addition to warrant a comment.

"What is that gold chain you wear, Uncle?" she asked.

He colored up red as a beet. "It is a lucky charm," he answered sheepishly.

"May I see it?"

"Just a little locket," he said, tucking it under the scarf. Clarence was never reluctant to show off a new acquisition. Quite the contrary. It was a wonder she hadn't been required to aid in the selection, as well as admire the thing.

She glanced quickly to her mother, who was shaking her head unobtrusively from side to side, indicating this line of questioning was not to be pursued. As soon as Clarence left, however—and he left very early these days—it reemerged.

"Mama, what is Uncle Clarence up to?" she demanded.

"I don't know, Prue, but I think he is involved with a woman. He has taken to using scent—you must have noticed."

"He was always very leery of women! He wouldn't paint one without a chaperone."

148

"You notice he no longer asks us to chaperone him. His moving into a studio was a bad move. I come to think he did it to avoid our knowing what he is up to."

Prudence was strongly of a mind to tell her mother what was being said. She desisted for two reasons. The worry of it might be hard on her health, but more importantly, she had taken the notion it was Lord Dammler who was responsible for the awful state of affairs. She would go to the studio. It had to be done, to see for herself just what sort of an ass Clarence was making of himself. She would go that very day.

Before she did it, however, she was the recipient of a call that put everything else out of her head. Lady Malvern came in person at eleven o'clock to give her an invitation to her literary house party at Finefields.

Constance was ravishing, as usual. Her black hair grew in a widow's peak and her face was exquisite, with those criminally beautiful violet eyes aglow. She was outfitted in a bonnet that surpassed even the expensive creations of Mademoiselle Fancot, and a suit that did justice to the bonnet. It was enough to make one despair to be in the same room with so much elegant good taste and beauty. But when the nature of the visit was outlined, there was little room for despair.

"Tom Moore tells me you have overcome your aversion to literary lions, Miss Mallow, and I hope you will do me the honor to join a little party I am throwing. You really must come—you have called off on me before, and owe me a visit. Your old friend Miss Burney will be there. Tom Moore, Mr. Rogers, old Sheridan, if he can make it. *Do* say you will come."

Prudence was enraptured. The Malverns were the apex of *ton*. To be included would return her to high society, where she felt a strong desire to be, not so much for the eminence as for the chance to see Dammler.

149

Not a single thought of the immorality of the crew occurred to her, though a party that included the likes of Fanny Burney was hardly likely to be dissolute. She longed to hear whether Dammler would be of the party, but disliked to ask outright.

As though reading her mind, Lady Malvern went on to raise the point. "Dammler can't make it, but then one hears he has lost an interest in literature."

That she had been speaking to Tom Moore was now evident. That Dammler had some new flirt under his patronage was equally evident, but why in the world was he drawing *Clarence* into the affair? If he wanted his lady's likeness taken, why not go to a real artist? It looked almost like revenge.

Prudence accepted the invitation, which entailed a busy week of arranging a toilette to do it justice, but she did not quite forget Clarence's studio in her rush. She cornered him the next morning over breakfast.

"When are you going to take Mama and myself to see your studio, Uncle?" she asked.

"Any time you like."

"Good, I should like to go today. I shall drop in this afternoon. I have some shopping to do, and shall stop by then."

"No!" he said at once. Too fast, too loud, too horrified!

She looked at him in alarm. "You said any time."

"I must have a warning. That is—there are any number of men hanging around watching me work. The place is always cluttered up with young bucks. I will want to clear the riffraff out of my atelier before you come."

"Tomorrow, then." Not that it would serve the purpose. She wanted to catch him unawares, and was sorry she had given a hint of her plan. That foreign atelier confirmed Dammler's hand in it.

"No." Less fast, less loud, less horrified, but very firm. "I have a special model I am working on."

"Who is that?"

"No one you would know. She is very shy, and doesn't like to have anyone but her patron watching when I paint her."

So much for the crowd of wild bucks! "Who is her patron?" Prudence asked.

"You wouldn't know him either!"

"What sort of a woman has a *patron,* Clarence?" Wilma asked suspiciously.

"A professional woman," he answered vaguely.

"What is her profession?" Prudence demanded. But she knew the answer. The oldest profession in the world; the woman was a prostitute. She also had strong suspicions as to the identity of the patron.

"She is an actress. A very serious actress, you know, like Mrs. Jordan."

"You never mean the Duke of Clarence is there in your studio!" Mrs. Mallow asked.

"Damne, I didn't say it *was* Mrs. Jordan. Someone like her, but prettier."

This sent the women scanning the great dramatic actresses of the day, but it soon sent Prudence right back to Lord Dammler. It was probably Mrs. Tempest, the woman who played *Shilla* in the play!

They could get no name from him. He became quite testy when they persisted. Prudence by no means gave up on discovering the secret. She could hardly go in person when the atelier was a hang-out for such persons and when she had been told firmly not to, but there was nothing to prevent her taking a stroll past the studio every time she was downtown, and she was there three days in a row with all the items to be bought to wear at Finefields. The studio, unfortunately, was on the second story, so that she couldn't even peek in the window. She could see without the aid of a window, though, that there was heavy traffic in and out. The model seemed to be shy only of female viewers; all the gayest bucks of the town were there. On the third day, she saw as well that Dammler's curricle was standing by. It was easily recognizable by the tigerskin coverings on the seats. Prudence made three passes in front of the studio that day, timed at roughly half-hour intervals. The curricle was still there on her last trip. It was either Mrs. Tempest, or the girl he had been buying a bonnet at Mademoiselle Fancot's. She didn't think it was the latter. She wasn't gaudy enough.

14

Prudence had become so intrigued with the goings-on at her uncle's studio that she was reluctant to leave town, even for a visit to Finefields with the most interesting crew London could throw up. She knew Dammler was not to attend, but that, for once, was not the real sore point. She had given up on reclaiming him. Her aim now was to prevent his ruining Clarence. The mystery of the charm around his neck continued to engross her. The little locket had been seen to fall out of the open neck of his shirt more than once. It was a small, round locket, just as he claimed, but what was in it? Once he even opened it when he sat across the room from her. He had looked at it with a bemused smile, then with an audible sigh closed it up. It had something to do with a woman. Of that she was sure. Men didn't wear that fatuous, foolish smile for any other purpose. Had Clarence fallen under the spell of a fair charmer? It looked powerfully like it, but then if the woman were Dammler's flirt, Clarence could hardly hope to compete.

Her mother was drawn in to assist in getting a look at the locket. She hadn't much better luck than Prudence, for it never left his body, but she had been at his elbow once when it fell open, and she thought there was a lock of hair in it—a curl. A blond curl. Prudence already knew the charm involved a woman. One who was either a blonde, a redhead or a brunette, so this added little knowledge. It did arouse a suspicion, but when she quizzed her mother she could not say that the blond curl was platinum.

"Marjorie, his wife, was a blonde," Wilma said hopefully.

"Yes," Prudence said—but so was Cybele a blonde, and Clarence never spoke of his late wife from one year's end to the next.

The matter was still unresolved when she set out for Finefields in Mr. Moore's well-sprung chaise. Clarence was not to be parted from his carriage at all these days, nor would the high perch phaeton have done her much good for a long trip, in any case. She was always required to hire a cab, but for the long trip, Mr. Moore had offered to deliver her.

It was an excellent gathering. Finefields offered the optimum in comfort and elegance, and at this particular time, the best of society in Miss Mallow's view. She renewed acquaintance with Miss Burney in the mornings, discussed books and writing with her. Miss Burney was getting on in years, but a lady who had enjoyed the society of Dr. Johnson, been keeper of the robes to the Queen and been interned by Napoleon of France due to her marriage to a French general must always be an interesting talker. In the afternoons they went for walks and drives about the estate with an assortment of companions. The dinners in the evening were beyond anything Prudence was accustomed to, yet for all this she had no feeling of being above herself. With the single exception of Lady Malvern, there were no dauntingly beautiful or elegant females present. A leftover trousseau served very well, along with the bits of garniture bought to dress it up. Three days passed so pleasantly that Clarence and the locket were slipping to the back of her mind. Not out of it entirely, but to the rear for consideration upon her return to London.

They had arrived on Friday. Tuesday morning the

group was at the table taking a leisurely breakfast when the mail was brought in. This was a part of the routine. On this occasion, Prudence was surprised to receive a letter herself, forwarded by her mother. It was not an important document, from an ex-neighbor back home, but it lent a cosy feeling, to be sitting opening and perusing a letter amongst this prestigious crew. Lady Malvern generally received an impressive stack of letters, as she did this day. She flipped through them, lifting out one with some interest to scan over quickly. She looked pleased when she set it down, then glanced to Prudence with a questioning look.

"A note from Dammler. He means to look in on his way to Longbourne. He goes there tomorrow—no, today. Tuesday, he says. He usually stops off on his way by to bait his horses. He says he wants to speak to you, Mr. Moore, about something or other. How nice. We shall ask him to dinner."

"Good!" Moore answered. "I have been looking him up without success for a week. He has been making himself too scarce of late."

Prudence waited to hear Mr. Rogers introduce the subject of painting, but he had been prodded to reticence by Moore and the hostess. Not another word was said on the subject. It was to be treated as a matter of no importance then. She must accept it as a social trifle like the others.

"Miss Mallow and I are off to your excellent library, Constance," Miss Burney said, intimately aware of what Prudence must be feeling. "We are interested in looking up that set of letters by Horace Walpole you have. They are not in circulation, I think you mentioned. I should adore to see them."

Prudence was grateful for the woman's tact, and happy to get into the quiet of the library to ponder how she should proceed. She wondered if Dammler knew she was there, or if it was Constance that brought him. That he came to see Moore never so much as entered her head, though it was the truth.

Dammler hadn't the faintest notion Prudence was at Finefields. Not a word could he get out of Clarence on her doings, and quizzing was difficult with the throng always in the atelier. Nor was he interested in Constance either. For a few confused weeks he had dabbled a bit in physics and the novel, then become interested in Clarence's studio. He first hoped Prudence would turn up there to see for herself that Miss Penny was her uncle's model. He realized as the audience grew that there was no likelihood of that, but was too unsettled to write. He often spent an hour in the afternoon with Clarence, watching him daub away and explain all his new techniques. Lately, he spent more than an hour. Cybele had never ceased to attract Clarence. Again and again, he was pestered to arrange for her to pose for Clarence. Ever versatile, he had a million excuses to fob him off. Exxon wouldn't allow it. Then Clarence learned from some other watchers that Exxon was gone home to his estate in Warwick, and it seemed the ideal time for it, to get it over with. Still disliking to do it, he claimed the Rembrandt style wouldn't suit her.

"I know that! Obviously she must be done as Venus, in the style of Botticelli. I have thought it all out. There's no shell in the world large enough for her to stand on, of course, and her hair ain't long enough to trail around her body—'Birth of Venus,' of course, will be the picture. Venus floating along the water on her shell, with Miss Penny and another gel from the theater to hold the cape and blow wind on her. I'll stand her on a chair, and paint up a big picture of a shell, using a

156

small one for a model. No trouble in it. Here, I have the cartoon sketched up in the way I mean to do her."

A tracing of Botticelli's "Birth of Venus" was thrust into Dammler's hands. "I'm afraid Exxon wouldn't like it," he insisted, determined to leave it at that.

Cybele, however, heard of the new artist from her sister actresses, and was eager to be painted for posterity. Much she cared for Exxon! She was through with him. A much more dashing buck was ogling her, and besides, Exxon was always pestering her to drop out of the play. She adored tha play. To be wearing the pretty chiffon costumes, and a black wig and dancing! It was like a party every night. And they paid her for it, too. With Clarence shouting in one ear and Cybele wheedling in the other, Dammler gave in and brought her to the studio, where Clarence, within the space of three seconds, realized he had finally met the woman to replace his late wife.

He would marry her. But first he would paint her half a dozen times. She would be Venus rising from the waves, and she would be Mona Lisa with that tantalizing smile. She would be Mary Magdalene and the Virgin Mary, as well, but Dammler knew nothing of all these plans. He saw Clarence was hypnotized by the girl, and sat faithfully protecting him till Venus had risen from the waves. She was such a troublesome model he never thought Clarence would tackle her again. Like a child, she required constant amusement. Work must stop while he procured ices for her. She brought her little pug along, to pester Clarence to distraction with his yapping and heel-nipping. She babbled and giggled throughout the sessions, never standing still a minute, and all the while Clarence fell deeper and deeper in love. When the first picture was finished, Dammler realized he had been wasting a good

157

deal of time, and with a guilty conscience decided that as he couldn't write, he would go to Longbourne Abbey and oversee estate matters. Constance had invited him to her house party, and while he had no thought of wasting a week *talking* about writing, he would spend an afternoon with Moore, his old friend, and take him some notes he wanted on the east. He mistakenly thought Clarence's long face indicated a disenchantment with Cybele, and hadn't a single worry on that score when he left the city.

He went off to Finefields pretty well resigned to making a life for himself that was worthwhile and very dull. Why must the two go together? It could have been worthwhile and interesting with Prue.

Knowing he was coming, Prudence contrived to be well away from the house by late afternoon, when he was believed to be arriving. She took a run into the closest village with Miss Burney and Mr. Moore, to see what authors the bookshop was carrying. The expressed purpose was to buy a pair of silk stockings for Miss Burney, but they all three turned in at the first bookstore without the need of a word being spoken. It seemed an unnecessarily cruel prank on the shopkeeper's part that Dammler's *Cantos from Abroad* should reside side-by-side with *Babe in the Woods* mocking her and causing Burney and Moore to exchange a secret, laughing smile. The works of Miss Burney were also on prominent display, as was Mr. Moore's *The Two-penny Post Bag,* so that the trip was thought to be well worthwhile despite the forgetting of the stockings.

Till dinnertime, Prudence kept away from Dammler, though she saw the tigerskin-seated curricle in the stable, and knew he was there. By then he had learned as well of her presence, had had time to wonder if she thought he was chasing her, and to determine he would show by his manner it was nothing of the sort. He considered an outrageous flirtation with Constance, made more difficult by the fact she had her latest conquest always at her heels; a very high-toned philosophical evening with Tom to show her how far beneath himself and the others she ranged intellectually, and lastly to get right down to it and wonder whether she would speak to him at all after the episode in the hatshop. He still hadn't set on his course when he went below a quarter of an hour before dinner, to find her sitting with Fanny Burney in the saloon, sipping sherry and wondering together how they had forgotten the silk stockings. Tom Moore was with them, which provided Dammler an excellent reason—even Prudence couldn't call it an excuse—to join them. He had come here for the sole purpose of speaking to Tom.

"Tom, I have been meaning to call on you," Dammler said, walking to the sofa, nodding with an impartial smile to Tom and the two ladies, who nodded back in unison, like a pair of Siamese cats, Prudence thought.

"Thought you was dead," Moore said in reply. "Sent half a dozen notes around to your place, and never got an answer from any of them."

"You know I'm a shockingly bad correspondent, but I have the notes with me—the ones you asked about in your letters. What is it you're writing that has to do with details of oriental splendor? Planning to invade my territory and do something on the east?"

Miss Burney replied lightly, "If we any of us stray from a polite English saloon, Dammler, we are invading your territory. You write about the whole world."

"Very true, but I don't do it nearly so well as Tom. Just what is it you're planning to write, Tom?" he asked, turning back to the man, to indicate who in the circle had drawn him.

"A hodgepodge thing—narrative verses set in the Orient, held together like raisins in a bun by a wad of prose. *Lalla Rookh,* I call it."

"Ah ha, about a lady, I see. More stealing from Dammler."

"Oh, I thought it must be about a blackbird—a rook," Miss Burney intruded.

Dammler decided to let her join their discussion. "It is a name, Fan. *Lalla Rookh* is a name."

"Daughter of an emperor, she is," Tom added. "I set her off on a voyage as Fielding did with his character in *Joseph Andrews,* to while away the time on the trip with stories as Chaucer did in his *Canterbury Tales.* I borrow from all the very best sources, you see—Dammler, Fielding and Chaucer."

"You'll mix up a better pudding than any of us," Dammler said generously. "And now it's time for you to ask me what *I* am doing."

This had, to Prudence at least, the sound of an announcement. She listened without saying a word to hear it. "Hear you're taking up painting," Moore said in a quiet aside.

Dammler frowned him down, then proceeded. "I am going into politics," he said. "My literary inspiration has deserted me, and I have been talked into introducing a bill in Parliament by Lord Holland." The speech, once out, struck him as disasterous. "To Prudence, my inspiration," was before his eyes, in letters two feet high. He daren't glance towards her.

"Oh, Dammler, no!" Miss Burney lamented. "How can you say so, when your love sonnets are so widely acclaimed? They were marvelous. Any old prose-talker can introduce a bill in Parliament. You must continue writing your poetry."

The love sonnets were not even officially out. He fell

160

deeper and deeper into shame with every utterance, to hear them spoken of as "widely acclaimed." "Oh, they were drivel—puerile ramblings I did well to suppress," he said quickly, then thought that was ill-advised, too. Prue was the inspiration; to suggest they were puerile might lead her to believe he had outgrown the sentiments, which was not at all what he meant to convey.

"They were excellent," Moore took it up. "Nonsense to hold them back, but about politics, my lad, leave it to the professionals. It is no place for a babe in the woods like you." Even this harmless suggestion must contain the title of her book! And used wrongly too, as she had used it herself. Probably *not* wrongly, if Tom said it. Language grew, changed subtly. "But did I not hear you are writing a novel?" Tom asked.

"No," he answered. Prudence looked at him in surprise. He couldn't even answer a question today. "That is, I tried my hand at it, but found it impossible. I leave the field to the ladies, and of course Mr. Scott, the best of them all." Oh, God! Why did he have to add that last, with *two* novelists staring at him.

"He is very condescending, is he not, Miss Mallow?" Miss Burney continued on in her playful vein. *"Poetry* is beyond our poor talents, you see. We are to leave *it* for the gentlemen, while we vex ourselves with the inferior chore of constructing mere novels, in emulation of Mr. Scott. Of course we daren't aspire to equal *him!"*

"I didn't mean anything of the sort!" he exclaimed in chagrin. "I couldn't do it to save my soul. It requires too much planning and thinking. Poetry you have only to *feel,* a novel must be thought out as well."

"There was a good deal of thought in your latest sonnets, I think," Fanny continued.

"No, I felt them and transposed my thoughts to paper."

"Without the intervening step of words having to be sorted out. I see how it is. It was done under the influence of opium, like Mr. Coleridge's *Kubla Khan*. We must try that technique, Miss Mallow. It will save us a deal of thinking. Shall we go and have a cup of opium? Or do you recommend a pipe, Lord Dammler?" Fanny asked roguishly.

"I don't recommend it at all, ma'am. The use of drugs at least has never been laid in my dish." This speech displeased him as much as the others. There was an inference in it that he had had all the other shattered commandments attributed to him. And why did Prudence sit there like a damned oyster, pretending to take no interest in the talk? He straightened his shoulders and turned towards her purposefully.

"How does *Patience* go on, Prudence?" he asked.

"We two dull virtues plod on as ever. I should perhaps add a little of your vice to liven it up."

As bad as all the rest! The whole crew were out to roast him. "I can well spare it," he answered with a cocky laugh that hid entirely his growing anger. "Which of my sorts do you think would add the right flavor? Drunkenness, sloth, avarice?"

"It was none of those I had in mind," she answered offhandedly, and turned to Fanny, but he was not about to let her off the hook.

"No? Which have I omitted? You must let me know, so that I can get on with the job of ruining myself in good earnest."

"You don't appear to need any help in that pursuit, Lord Dammler."

He glared at her, but Moore jumped in to forestall disaster. "Rogers is here somewhere. He has been lying in for four weeks, and has lately had the midwife in to deliver a couplet. Such a chore it is for him. He'll want to be congratulated on it. Be sure you ask him how the delivery went. Ah, there he is off in the corner by himself, sulking. Come along, Allan, we'll inquire for the infant's health. Excuse us, ladies." He got Dammler by the elbow and took him away, with just one angry glance at Prudence.

"Dammler can be quite the most charming man, but he is a sadly unstable character, don't you think?" Miss Burney asked.

"He is very excitable," Prudence answered mildly. She had found him more exciting than excitable. He had got her so excited she could hardly speak, and knew she wouldn't be able to eat a bite of dinner—done it with no more than a glance and a few jibes. If he took into his head to come to cuffs with her, she would claim a migraine and go straight to her bed. He would know she was lying too, and say so to the whole group.

15

Lady Malvern had to do some juggling of her seating arrangement with the arrival of Dammler for dinner. Satisfied with her own current flirt, a Sir Lyle Wharton, she gave the poet to Fanny Burney. It was a dreadful waste to place him next a lady in her sixties, but, till she saw how they went on together these days, she would not inflict him on Miss Mallow, and he was too fast for her country guests. Fanny regaled him very satisfactorily over dinner with an account of her internment in France by Napoleon. So well, in fact, that he returned to her side when the gentlemen finished their port and joined the ladies in the gold saloon. That she was sitting with Prudence, as she usually was, was no reason he shouldn't continue a particularly lively discussion they had been engaged in at the meal's end.

He took up a chair at Miss Burney's end of the sofa and said at once, "I think it a particularly barbarous custom that the ladies are shunted off to the saloon just when the meal is over, and some decent conversation is possible."

"It is but one of the barbarous customs perpetrated against us," Mis Burney replied, quite flattered at his attentions. She had of course no interest of a romantical nature in him, but always liked to be on terms with her fellow writers, and the best way to be on terms with Dammler was to provide a good argumentative partner in whatever he was in a mood to discuss.

"No, really! It is we men who suffer by it. I daresay you and Miss Mallow have been having an enlightened discourse on some matter of interest, while I have been subjected to an hour of politics."

"Subjected! But surely you said not two hours ago that you meant to take the subject up full time," Fanny pointed out.

He laughed uneasily, seeing that he was falling right back into idiocy, as soon as he was in Prue's company again. "Caught me dead to rights! But I consider the new career as a duty. Very likely writing will remain my avocation. You were just telling me something about a cathedral in France, Fan, when you left."

"Are you really interested in discussing *churches*, Dammler?" she asked with an arch smile.

"I am interested in massive architecture of all sorts," he replied, refusing to recognize any slur on his morals in this shot. To fill the silence he went on with some interests in this line. "After having seen the Sphinx in Egypt, for instance, the Colosseum at Rome and the Parthenon in Greece, one is at a loss to imagine how they were constructed so long ago, with no knowledge of modern engineering. I doubt we could reproduce such mammoth things today in England, with all our technology."

A few timid glances towards Prudence were attempted during this speech, and at its end his eyes settled on her, to include her in the discussion.

"I don't know about today, but something similar was done in the past, was it not, at Stonehenge?" she asked, rather tentatively.

"Ah, Stonehenge!" he took it up eagerly. "A queer thing, a real mystery, those great monoliths standing in the middle of Salisbury Plain. Extraordinary! I often think of them when I see the lords standing around the grate at the House, talking mystical nonsense."

"I suppose they were some sort of place of worship in

their day," Prudence suggested hesitantly, for she had no great interest in or knowledge of antiquity.

"A church, you mean?" he asked, with the greatest interest. "Why do you say so?" It was not his intention to be argumentative, but only to keep the conversation ball rolling in this inoffensive groove.

"Only because such a huge undertaking must have been inspired by religious motives. If you look at the ruins of antiquity, the Parthenon dedicated to Athena, the Temple of Nike and so on, all were religious buildings. Man requires an awe-inspiring reason to so exert himself." Prue looked to Miss Burney for support, and received a silent nod of agreement.

"The Colosseum had no such inspiration," Dammler pointed out. "It was built for purposes of the most bloodthirsty sport and entertainment. In many other cases you will find self-defense to have been the motivating force. Survival is man's strongest instinct. All the fortress castles scattered about the countryside of Europe, as well as Hadrian's Wall and the Great Wall of China bear me out."

"Oh walls, that is something quite different," Prudence said quickly, wishing they might change the subject. "I spoke of *buildings*. Naturally a *wall* would not be used for worship."

"They would be surprised to hear it in Jerusalem, where the Wailing Wall is usually pretty well occupied on Fridays with Jews lamenting and praying." She gave him a vexed, frustrated look. It was an uneven match, that he who had traveled the world should choose his travels to argue about. He saw the signs of withdrawal on her countenance, and hastened on to contradict himself. "Of course it is on the site of Solomon's Temple, a remnant of the great temple built by Herod, and has churchlike associations."

"Normally an ordinary wall would not be used for worship you must own, Dammler," Miss Burney said with a laugh.

"I do admit it, and neither are most huge buildings, either. Those that weren't built for defense were built for a woman, nine-tenths of them."

"A woman? How can you say so?" Fanny asked, astonished.

"How can a sane man say anything else? Look at the Taj Mahal, built by a Mogul emperor for his favorite wife, Mumtaz Mahal."

"You will observe he keeps track of the lady's name, but not the emperor's," Miss Burney said in a playful spirit to Prudence.

"Shah Jehan was the uxorious gentleman's name," Dammler said, smiling. "But he's long gone, Fan. There is no hope of your getting a castle from him."

"It is news to me if one example proves a case. It is the exception rather than the rule," Prudence said in a damping way that renewed Dammler's attack.

"How many examples do you require, ma'am? There is the Petit Trianon, and not so *petit,* either, built by Louis Quinze for his favorite mistress, Pompadour."

"You tread on dangerous ground when you go to France, Dammler. You forget I have some familiarity with it," Fanny pointed out. "All the cathedrals there, the great gothic cathedrals, were built for worship."

"Called Notre Dame, everyone of them," he said with a quizzing smile.

"*Called* Notre Dame, for the Virgin, but *built* for worshipping God. That proves our point, does it not?"

"It proves that in France there exists a great respect for the Virgin. I speak in terms of religion only, you understand," he added with a dangerous sparkle that warned Prudence he was about to become even more outrageous.

But, with Fanny to shoulder the burden of outwitting him, she entered into the discussion, and began to take some pleasure in it. "In any case, we have established most churches were built for purposes of worship, and that was our point," she said.

"No, you have surely lost track of the point," he contradicted baldly. "I will go you a step better and concur that *all churches* were built for worship. It is redundant to say so, a church being by definition a place of divine worship, but it is large buildings in general that we are discussing."

"I cannot think Stonehenge in any case was built for a woman," Fanny said. "Who in her right mind would want such a weird thing?"

"Oh but women and a sound mind don't usually go together," Dammler said, smiling broadly now to indicate this was mere persiflage. "We'll find out when the archaeologists get around to solving the riddle that some demanding wench wanted a larger colonnade than her neighbor, or a backdrop for her garden."

"Something new in the world, a garden of such dimensions," Prudence said.

"There is nothing new under the sun. One of the seven wonders of the *ancient* world, you will recall, was the Hanging Gardens of Babylon. They would dwarf the monoliths of Stonehenge. Built by Nebuchadnezzar, at the behest of his queen, no doubt. You will notice I can't supply the lady's name, Fan."

"Not even *one* doubt he built it for his own greater glory?" Miss Burney asked.

"Not in *my* mind. Men are all fools about pretty women. The pages of history are littered with our corpses, beggaring, wounding, even killing ourselves

168

to please you tiresome creatures." He rubbed his shoulder and leveled a meaningful look on Prudence, who hadn't a notion what he was getting at.

"I have usually found the pages of history littered with the corpses of men killing themselves to usurp a country that doesn't belong to them," she pointed out, very much in the spirit of her discussions with Allan at home in Grosvenor Square. She was beginning to wish Fanny Burney would discover some other party to go to.

"Or a woman that doesn't belong to them," Dammler pointed out, wagging a slender finger at her. "*Vide* Helen of Troy."

It was Fanny who found an answer, however. "It is not established that the Trojan War was fought over Helen. There is myth and legend so mixed up in it—well, Eros, the Goddess of Discord . . ."

"And love," Dammler added quickly. "But then the two are practically inseparable. Sorry for the interruption."

"Eros is supposed to have been instrumental in starting it, so you cannot call it *history*."

"Myth based on fact, as myths usually are. They found the right culprit in a woman, in any case. You have only to look at literature—you don't see Hero being so foolish as to swim the ice-cold Hellespont for Leander. No sir, a man making an ass of himself and as often as not getting killed, for the love of a woman, every time." Prudence received another reproachful look, but took it as an indictment of her sex. "Cleopatra making fools of Caesar and Mark Antony, and even in the Bible, Delilah shearing Samson down to size. Salome—the word means *'peace,'* imagine!—ordering up poor John's head on a platter, and Herod so infatuated he did it for her, too. Why, there is nothing a beautiful

169

woman might not do once she has laid her conscience to rest."

"I am stunned into silence at such a plethora of evidence of our fallen nature," Fanny laughed.

"You, Prudence, nothing to say in defense of your sex?" he asked with a certain pointedness.

"I expect what has been robbing you and me of a monument all these years, Miss Burney, is our conscience," she answered.

"Oh, have you grown one of those?" he asked, with a little laugh. "I daresay Salome felt a twinge when she saw John's head coming in."

"He works by induction," Prudence explained to the other lady, quite easy in her mind now. "He goes from the specific to the general, you see, which is never conducive to fact, only more or less to probability. You will notice he avoids *deduction*. It is the university teaches gentlemen these sly tricks to confuse us women."

"What, you refuse to believe the evidence of history when it is at such pains to repeat itself, *ad nauseam?* Would you like more examples? Let us quit trifling and begin at the beginning of our own species. Take Adam and Eve now, a typical case of man betrayed, and everyone of you since has followed in Eve's footsteps."

"More induction!" Prudence cautioned. Yet as she cast hurriedly about in her mind for some refutation, she could think of no good female except Hannah More, and she seemed sadly out of place in this historical and Biblical discussion. "There was Queen Elizabeth!" she announced at last. "Look at all the good she did, and without benefit of a king, too, I might add."

"By all means let us take Liz. A typical example. How did she go on now? Had her cousin Mary executed, killed her lover, Exeter, carried on quite shamelessly with all her courtiers, using them for her own ends,

170

including poor Sir Walter Raleigh, whom she ultimately tossed into the Tower when she'd finished with him, and in a dirty coat, too. A typically heartless, selfish female. Only think what she might have accomplished if she hadn't been as ugly as our present Queen! Yes, she is really an excellent argument on *my* side, ladies, but how about *yours?*"

"Now he has sunk to roasting us," Fanny said. "I have every assurance you can handle Dammler without my help, Miss Mallow, and I see Malvern is beckoning me to the card table, so I leave this sophist in your capable hands."

"Now we get down to an equal match," he said, smiling with satisfaction as he arose to join her on the sofa, with a light of anticipation in his eyes.

Prudence feared the match had become suddenly very uneven indeed, but was not about to let him know it. Nor did she feel the slightest dread he meant to be impossible. He was the old Dammler again, lively, engaging, and still the most interesting man she had ever met. "It astonishes me to learn you hold such a low opinion of females," she said with a happy martial light glowing in her eye.

"You know me better than that, Prudence! I am as eager as the next to be made a fool of by a beautiful woman. Come, do your worst. It won't be the first time you've decked me out in cap and bells, to play the clown."

"You play Don Juan more convincingly."

"The greatest clown in history—I am a natural for the role. And will be delivered unto devils like Don one day; meanwhile, I am at your disposal to deliver to a more temporal fate. Or do I offend you, to intimate my role as 'Guelph' will not be immortal?"

How quickly all her dread returned as he delivered

this sentence. She looked up, alert to danger, to see him quizzing her with his best smile. "But I forgive you," he went on. "The male of the species—what chance have I against a woman? It is your custom to prey on us. Futile to fly in the face of nature. And in return we glorify you."

It was not raw nature he spoke of, but the novel and the sonnets. They were getting down to it, and she was half glad. "I have told you I am sorry about that."

"I have told you I forgive you. Let us not become repetitive. We were used to argue more fiercely."

Eager to be done with personalities, she turned to more objective matters. "Ah, well, if it is an argument you are after, I shall be happy to oblige you. I have been making use of the dull repetition time in my usual prudent fashion to gather my wits and present you with the following point. If it weren't for us women, much as you deride our selfishness, the world would be bereft of massive architecture. To say nothing of the other arts—painting, sculpture, poetry."

"Very true. I have been saying for some time we exert our best efforts to immortalize you. Mona Lisa, Clarence's old flirt, Heloise, Phryne—who would ever have heard of any of them if a man hadn't written about them, or painted them? What is known of La Gioconda but that Leonardo thought her face worthy of recording? I fail to see the attraction myself—a very sly smile the lady wears. Or of a little French orphan if Abelard hadn't fallen desperately in love with her and renounced a career that might have seen him Pope, to say nothing of other *disastrous* physical consequences for his pains?"

"Well, but on the other hand, who would have heard of the men, if women hadn't inspired them to greatness?"

"I have an inkling we might have heard of Leonardo

without Lisa. He did a few other things, you know. However, it was *my* point that men exert themselves to the limit for a woman. Somehow, you end up supporting me every time. Do you think it could be because I am right?"

"No, I think it is probably because *you* have ten thousand books, while *I* have only two small shelves. Lady Malvern has more, however, and tomorrow I shall browse through them and discover who these Heloises and Phrynes are you speak of. Unless you wish to enlighten me now? I confess you know more cold facts that I do."

"More hot ones, too, I bet!" he laughed, then sobered up quickly. "Oh, dear, how did I come to mouth so much debauchery in two minutes? Neither a castrated cleric nor a Greek prostitute can be of any interest to you, Prudence."

She felt a sudden twinge of guilt that he was again muddying her with his black character. Yet how nice it was to hear him talk, knowledgeably and well about something of more interest to her than Clarence and his interminable painting. How long was it since a conversation with anyone had sent her to the library to learn a new fact?

For some time they talked on about objective matters, not touching again on the state of affairs between themselves, but reaching at least a superficial peace. It was impossible to remain isolated all evening at a polite house party, however, and later Mr. Rogers and some others joined them.

When Prudence went up to her bed, a ridiculously ornamental affair more closely resembling a gazebo or pleasure dome than a canopy, she was still excited from the encounter. Allan had not seemed so very angry about the book. Why had he stayed away for so

173

long? But they had not really spoken at length on personal matters. Another day, she thought, might bring that about. What should she do if he was inclined to offer for her again? Throw her scruples to the wind and snatch at the chance, as she wanted to, or be wise. "An unstable character," Fanny had called him, and it was true. Yet how attractive an unstable character was to her, when he came in the form of Lord Dammler.

16

The habits of a lifetime were not broken so easily
that Prudence actually stayed in her bed past eight in
the morning. She went down to breakfast at nine-
thirty or ten like the others, but it meant dallying in
her chamber for the better part of two hours. Today she
would dally in the library, instead, to gain fuel for her
discussions with Allan. She smiled happily as she
roamed the shelves, peering into books of Grecian
antiquity and Egyptian monuments, architecture and
history—all matters that interested her because they
interested him. Surely that was a point to ponder, that
a man, even one who was not uniformly steady in character, should be the means of one continuing with her
education. A small voice told her there was nothing to
prevent her following a course of instruction apart
from Dammler, but a louder one told her she wouldn't
do it.

He was still not at the table when she finally went
into the breakfast parlor. Again there was a letter for
her, from her mother this time, with some unsettling
news. Clarence was behaving oddly, worse than before.
He now absented himself in the evenings as well as the
days, and Mrs. Mallow had taken alarm that it was a
female that took him away, as he would tell her nothing about his activities. Mrs. Hering had heard from
Sir Alfred, and considered the item of enough importance to involve relaying; that he had been seen on the
strut with a very beautiful woman, *young* woman. The
business was gone beyond sittings in a studio. He was

going public in the matter, and it caused Prudence some worry.

She was frowning into her letter when Dammler came to the table. "What's the matter, Prue?" he asked, stopping beside her.

She hastily stuffed the letter into her pocket. "Nothing serious. Mama is a little worried about Uncle. That's all."

Dammler did not look at all surprised at this, she noticed, and suspected he knew well about it. "Slipped the leash, has he?"

"It looks like it."

"We'll talk later," he said, looking around and finding he must move to the end of the table to take a seat.

Miss Burney began mentioning a drive over to see some church, but before a firm companion could be obtained in Miss Mallow, Lady Malvern said, "How long do you plan to remain with us, Dammler? I hope you won't rush off." As he and Prudence were not bickering, she considered it eligible to encourage him to remain.

"I must be at Longbourne today. I sent word I am coming. I'll have to leave soon."

"It's only a few hours away. Stay for lunch, at least."

"I want to talk to Tom this morning," he said, with a little questioning look to Prudence, that relayed he also wanted to talk to her.

The church Fanny spoke of was close enough to insure their being back for lunch, and Prudence went with her, as she didn't wish to announce she sat around waiting for a moment of Dammler's time. She had very little idea what she had seen when she got back. She only knew that after lunch she would be with him, and she could hardly wait for the meal to be over.

He walked to her side as they left the room. "Let's go

176

out into the garden to talk," he suggested as the group broke up to inhabit various rooms, thus taking away the certainty of privacy.

The idea appealed to her, though there was a brisk autumnal breeze in the air. In the hallway, she took up her pelisse. "I'll take this, to ward off the cold," she said.

"There is no such a thing as cold, Prudence," he said with a strange smile.

"Indeed? The Eskimos will be surprised to hear it."

"No, I'm serious. There is physically no such a thing as cold. There is only a relative absence of heat."

"You are *not* serious, but only looking for an argument, and I have other crows to pull with you, so this ploy is not at all necessary."

"The matter can be argued for hours together. I've done it."

"Where did you find anyone foolish enough to humor you in this conceit? I hadn't realized you were gallivanting with morons. I should have easy work winning today's round. I wish you were right, but if you are, my study has not heard of this new turn of physics. It is penetrated with the most soul-destroying cold ever felt—or *imagined*."

She was too sensible to argue the matter; too sensible too to give in without an argument. He thought of her remark about her cold study, thought of the fine grate in her rooms at Longbourne Abbey and in London. He didn't consider it the propitious moment to mention them, but some trace of his thoughts was in his eyes as he took her arm and opened the gate from the rose garden into the park. "What matter is it you wish to argue then?" he asked.

"The *monstrous* lies you perpetrated against Miss Burney and myself last night. Now I suppose you will tell me there is no such a thing as a lie, but only an

177

absence of truth, which ill-bred persons like myself call by their plain old Saxon name, lie."

"Old English, actually, from *lyge,* you know."

"What's the difference?"

"About five hundred years, but I didn't mean to be petty."

She lowered her brows at him, and was treated to one of his insouciant shoulder hunchings. "You are allowing lies to exist, are you?" she enquired.

"We always allow females to deal artistically and inventively with the truth," he answered, taking her arm to stroll through a pebble walk, where statuary loomed above them. "I am shocked at your loose tongue, Prudence. Here I have been taking you for a properly reared young lady. If you didn't hide behind your petticoats I would be impelled to call you out for that accusation. It is typical of women; you know you have us at this disadvantage of chivalry, and can say or do anything without fear of retribution."

"Fine talking, milord. Just where are we heading, incidentally?"

"Beyond earshot of Hebe and her friends. You can't trust a crowd of drinkers to hold their tongues."

"Who is this intemperate crew you are worried about?" she asked, looking around the empty garden.

"You don't know the vile habits of Hebe, wine-bearer to the gods? The gray lady up above you there in a very improper state of undress, tilting her jug precariously, urging a drink on all her companions." He waved towards the statues, that stood on high columns. "Your education has become sorely neglected, my dear. Time I take it in hand for you again, introduce you to some of my ten thousand tomes."

This leading remark sent her scruples into a state of shock, but he was rattling on before she could form any

178

resolutions to be broken. "Let us get right on with the lessons. The gentleman with horns there beside Hebe is not a cuckolded husband, as you may be forgiven for thinking, but a rather inferior imitation of Michelangelo's Moses, the horns resulting from a bad translation of the Bible or some such thing. The original in Rome is much better." He drew her to a stop, and went on pointing out the other statues.

"The charming lady *au naturel* next Moses is some stone incarnation of Venus or Aphrodite, rendered so poorly it is impossible to tell whether she is copied from the original Greek, or is a third-hand job taken from the Roman copy. It is not only we dramatists who plagiarize, you see. A time-honored custom in the arts. That will come as news to Clarence's niece," he said with a bantering smile.

"Odd the way they are arranged—man and woman, like a polite dinner party. That would be Constance's idea. What do you suppose Venus finds to say to Moses as they stand there, side by side, through the ages? Has to remind him of the Commandments, I daresay. Thou shalt *not*, Moses! Keep thy cold hands to thyself!"

She was surprised into a spontaneous laugh, but felt she ought to be enjoining him to behave. "You forget they are frozen in stone. He couldn't lay a rude hand on her if he wanted. I doubt he would want to either, the law-giver himself."

"Don't forget he was raised by Pharaoh's daughter when she fished him out of the Nile. Environment will tell. I always suspect a layer down of laws myself. I think Moses probably had a whitewash job done on him by his biographer—himself. Yes, he was a scribbler like us when all's said and done, therefore a highly suspect fellow. At least the Pentateuch is attributed to him."

179

"Oh, Dammler!" she said in exasperation, "is *nothing* sacred to you?"

"Nothing written—the matter of a human agent being required to sort out the words makes me suspicious. In the beginning was the act, not the word."

As the next statue to be explained was Zeus, the perpetrator of too many crimes to go into, he abandoned the lesson. "Prudence, I've just had what Tom Moore would call a 'gorgeous notion'—one I plagiarized from Omar Khayyam."

"I tremble to hear it."

"A crock of wine, a loaf of bread and a gorgeous female in the wilderness. We'll pass on the bread, and see if we can't get Constance to provide the wine and wilderness." He beckoned to a gardener, and passed the interval till the wine came in selecting a private spot giving shelter without too much shade. When he had the wine and two glasses in his hand, he pointed off into the distance, so far from the house that she hesitated to go with him. She could not quite trust this mood he was in.

"I think I prefer the rose garden," she said.

"Not the primrose path? It's the wine you distrust. I'll get rid of it," he said at once, and lifted his arm to heave it away.

"Allan—no! Oh, you are outrageous," she said, but she went with him, laughing and happy in spite of all.

"I only want to talk to you alone. Come along, I promise I won't molest you. Word of a gentleman, and I *don't* lie, Miss Prudence."

She knew he referred to more than his present promise. He was telling her again he had been innocent of wrongdoing with Cybele. His meaningful look told her so.

They walked off into the park till they reached his

chosen corner. "Here, you won't want to dirty your pelisse," he said, pulling off his jacket to lay on the ground.

"Oh, no! It will ruin your nice jacket," she objected, while her eyes were treated to an equally nice flowered waistcoat, and a pair of shoulders that had no need of wadding to eke them out.

"Nonsense, chivalry isn't dead. I can be as gallant as Sir Walter Raleigh. Go on, step on it. I expect no better from a female."

"No really, it is too good to use as a blanket." She reached down to pick it up, but with a playful push on the shoulder he shoved her down.

"Do as you're told, woman. Sit. We don't read of Queen Liz refusing to tread Walter's coat into the mud." He then stuck the neck of the wine bottle to his mouth to extract the loosened cork with his teeth, while Prudence looked on in fascination. He poured the two glasses, balancing both in one hand. She felt as sinful as Salome should have when she reached out to take it.

"I want to propose a toast to all put-upon gentlemen everywhere, and the ladies who do the putting," he said, lifting his glass. "You don't drink to that, Miss Mallow? Compose one of your own."

"Oh, no. I'll drink to that. Behind every great genius there is a woman."

"Whispering in his ear he'll never make it. We forge on in spite, you see, to show the little woman we have it in us."

"I give you fair warning, Dammler, I have spent the early morning frolicking through Malvern's library, and am about to shoot all your cock-and-bull untruths down."

"Now that is a great compliment to me, that you took

181

my little jokes so seriously. *En garde!*" He held up his hand in a fencing gesture, and smiled with anticipation. "Go to it. You have first thrust."

She took a sip of wine and made her thrust. "Very well then, let us begin with the Taj Mahal in India. It turns out, upon investigation, it was built as a burial place for that old shah's wife, so I cannot believe she ever got much pleasure from it, or urged her husband on to do it. He probably beat her when she was alive, and only did it after her death to salve his conscience."

He nodded judiciously. "Still, he did it for her, not himself. God, but it's beautiful, Prue. I wish I could take you to see it—see it at night. It's like a great fairy castle, the white marble glowing in the moonlight. There is nothing in Europe to equal it."

"I consider that *my* point, all the same. Next we come to Madame Pompadour and her not so petit Petit Trianon."

"You'll have hard sledding to make anything of that expensive trollop."

"Still, on the lady's behalf let us point out she was a considerable patroness of the arts and learning, and gave Louis a pretty good hand in running the country. To each his just due. We give Prinney a pleasure dome at Brighton for making a worse mess than she did."

"No, sorry! I refuse to place Madame on the side of the angels. Let us couple her with Du Barry and her own sort. Not even half a point for you there. Next thrust."

"Very well then, Hero. Isn't that an odd name for a girl? You men stole it from her, but I sha'n't say a word about plagiarism or you'll lead me down the paths of etymology again. She threw herself into the Hellespont in a fit of grief and drowned when she heard of Leander's death, so you can't say *she* was heartless, or anything else but a confirmed ninnyhammer."

"That's two for you; one for me—but she's only legend, you know."

"Based on fact!"

"You have an excellent memory. Next?"

"Well, the books didn't say anything about Nebuchadnezzar building the gardens for his wife, so he is a moot point, and I win."

"You are jumping the gun, in typical female fashion. You have omitted Cleopatra."

"Oh she was the most abused of the lot!"

"She killed her own brother, who was also to be her husband. No accounting for taste."

"Only after he drove her into exile."

"What reason did you find for her setting up house with Caesar and Mark Antony?"

"She did it because she had to secure her empire, and besides, she probably loved them."

"You would allow that as an excuse for such a quantity of lovers, would you? Take care, your prudence is slipping," he said, smiling at her consternation at what she had said. "I made sure you'd finger Cleo as a sinner."

"Anyway, she killed herself when she heard Mark Antony was dead."

"Friend, Roman, Countrywoman! Lend me your ears!" He reached out and tweaked her ear. "She killed herself when she heard Octavian meant to take her to Rome in chains, which of course coincided with the death of Mark."

"You can't know that was the reason."

"You can't imagine it wasn't! I resort again to induction to make my own conclusion."

"I have got you at *point non plus,* in other words."

"You've talked yourself out on a limb, milady. Are you keeping score, by the by? That's two all, and now we come to the case of Lord Dammler versus Miss Mallow."

"It is presumptuous to include ourselves amongst the immortals," she said hastily.

"Immortal *lovers* we are discussing, Prue. Let us keep our terms straight."

She became flustered, and began looking with regret to the distance separating them from the house. "If you are talking about that dreadful book I wrote . . ."

"And my sonnets. Don't leave me out of it. I want a line in history, too."

"The circulation of your sonnets is hardly a phenomenon that will immortalize either of us, as you suppressed them."

"Terms, Miss Mallow. I insist on proper terminology. It was a noumenon—a non-event, devoid of actual occurrence. I make you a present of the word. I know you enjoy collecting them up."

"A noumenon is not likely to immortalize us in any case, is it?"

"It isn't really the sonnets I was hoping to discuss with you. Why didn't you come to see me after the duel?"

Regarding him, she noticed the evidences of offense on his face, and was unable to account for them. "It is more usual for the gentleman to call on a lady. I could hardly go trotting over to Berkeley Square alone."

"You might have come with Clarence. As I was bedridden, there could be no question of *my* going to *you*."

"Bedridden?" she asked, her eyes widening in astonishment. "I heard nothing of it. What was the matter? Were you ill?" His look told her she was wrong. "Allan, you never mean *you* fought the duel, after all?" she asked, totally dumbfounded.

"Didn't Clarence tell you?"

"Not a word! I had no idea at all. Oh, Allan, I'm sorry! But were you *wounded?* I hope it wasn't serious. Why didn't Uncle tell me?" The questions came tumbling out on top of each other.

"No, it wasn't serious, but I can't quite credit Clarence didn't let it slip out," he said, frowning at her.

"I promise you I had no idea! Oh, and *that* is why you didn't come."

She looked so humbled, so sorry, that the possibility of her being angry at his part in the duel was forgotten entirely. All was explained in a highly satisfactory way to Dammler.

"And that's why Hettie cut me dead. What must she think of me!" Prudence exclaimed.

"She thought you an unnaturally hardhearted woman, and so did I," he said, taking her hand eagerly.

"You know I would have been there if I'd known. Where were you hit? How serious was it? I didn't see you about for *weeks.*"

He rubbed his shoulder. "Just a scratch, but it became infected. I was in bed a week, and housebound for another, cursing you for a hussy the whole time. What did you think I was about last night, rhyming off all the female butchers to you and trying to look wounded?"

"I thought you were just showing off to Fanny."

"No, to you."

"Oh I'm surprised you should bother, if *that's* what you thought of me. Why didn't you *tell* me, Allan?"

"How could I ever imagine you didn't know? I felt sure Clarence would have told you all about it within five minutes."

They discussed it till Prudence knew the whole story, and she reached her own conclusions on her uncle's unwonted silence. "He was ashamed of himself, and well he might be! Oh, and there's another matter dealing with Uncle I must discuss with you. Who is the woman he is painting at his studio? Mama has taken the notion—she mentioned it in her letter today—that he has formed some sort of liaison with her. I *know* you know the whole, and I wish you will tell me."

"Not woman, women. There's safety in numbers. Actresses from Drury Lane. You saw one of them at Mademoiselle Fancot's the day I went with her to buy a feather, for *Clarence,* I might add. It seemed hard I should be given such a frigid shoulder for it, too."

"You arranged it for him, actresses from *Shilla?"*

"I got the first, and she sent along others. He pressed me to do it for him, but don't lay the atelier in my dish, if you please. He was all set up for business before he asked me to hire him a model—and it is only a *model* I arranged, Prue, not anything else, if that is the notion germinating in your head. I know what to think when your brow darkens up in that way."

Her brow lightened somewhat, but still she was worried. "You don't think he might go fancying himself in love with one of them?"

"Much good it would do him! The Mogul's ladies aim higher than a patron with two thousand pounds a year. Don't fret your head on that score."

"Still, he makes himself look ridiculous. People are laughing at him. I wish he hadn't done it. As you have been there during his painting sessions, tell me how he goes on. Is he a laughingstock?"

"He's happy as a dog in a sausage factory. I never saw him so merry."

"Yes, but is he making a fool of himself in public?"

"No, in the privacy of his own studio. Well it's not Clarence the men go to watch you may be sure. If he earns an occasional smirk, it is his right to make a bit of a fool of himself over the thing he loves. His art, I mean. He's too old for you to try to rule his life, Prue. He's your uncle, not your son. So a few fellows give a wink at his little folly— where's the harm? The audience is as foolish in my book."

"You are frequently in the audience, I assume?"

"I was there a few times, to keep an eye on him for you. He's enjoying himself immensely, and doing no one any possible harm. He's nudging sixty, having his last fling."

"I don't like his being seen on the streets with one of the models, as Mama said in her letter."

"That would be because *I* was not there to fetch and carry for him. He probably required some prop to dress one of the ladies up as a zephyr. It was a feather I was after when you saw me that day, but you will perhaps recognize it for a fern when you see his rendition of Rembrandt's Flora, or alternatively, a vine in a Botticelli."

"What, has he switched allegiance from Rembrandt, and he with two gallons of brown paint at home that will go to waste?"

"I believe I spotted a Leonardo amongst the canvases. Changing as fast as his models." He felt uneasy about one of the models, about Cybele, and toyed with the idea of mentioning her, but thought it gave too much significance for him to do so.

She felt some relief and said lightly, "I am dying to see the atelier, to view the new masterpieces."

"You must see them, but make your visit in his off hours, or you'll run into a bunch of females you would rather not know." Oh dear, and see Cybele perched on her shell, too. Have to get rid of that! He'd ask Clarence for it—buy it. Send him a letter that very day, to deliver it to Berkeley Square.

"Mmm, such as the little lady you were buying a feather," she added in a quizzing way. "And why is it, Lord Dammler, who speaks of a career in Parliament fritters away his afternoons amidst the lightskirts?"

"Because his inspiration deserted him. He found himself unable to write a word, equally unable to bear the solitude of his home without you." He squeezed her hand, bestowing a tentative, questioning smile on her.

"You lacked my presence behind you, whispering in your ear you'd never make it, in other words."

"Just so. All we geniuses require that sort of encouragement."

"One does not hear of Michelangelo ever having a woman behind him, or your old idol, Alexander Pope, or . . ."

"No!" he held up a hand. "I am *hoarse* de combat—verbal combat that is, and don't mean to pull that crow any more today."

"Still making those inferior bilingual puns," she smiled, shaking her head.

"Continue with the chorus. Don't forget to remind me they are the *lowest* form of humor, that being the standard refuge of those too slow-witted to make one themselves. Shakespeare felt, and I myself feel, differently, however."

"Harnessing yourself right up with William, I see."

"Certainly. Aim for the top. A man's reach must exceed his grasp, or what's a *meta* for?"

"Improving," she said, considering the word judiciously.

"I must confess it is a borrowing."

"Just *pun* ishment for your pride, to have to confess it," she said, peering up at him with a laughing sidewise glance.

"Prudence, you wretch! How *dare* you top me! That was my best one!"

"No, you could do much better if you weren't so *punctilious*. All right, I'll stop!" she squealed, as he began to close his fingers around her throat in a playful rendition of murder. "I'm glad you promised to behave!"

"It is all that saves you," he said in a menacing voice, but those glowing eyes looking into hers promised a fate from which she had not the least desire to be saved.

She reached up to pull his hands away, and he grabbed at them hastily. "It's been so good to talk to you again, Prue. That is what I miss most of all, your sweet siren call in my ear—you're a damned fool. And so am I, about you. May I call when I get back to London?"

"If the House of Parliament and the actresses can spare you for an hour, I should be delighted to receive you."

"Why don't you come with me to Longbourne?" he asked impulsively. "You've never been there."

"Allan! You know I can't go there with you alone."

"We'll bring Fanny Burney along to play propriety. She'd love to come, and I must confess I grow to like her better as I get to know her."

"I'm not ready for another trip. I am promised to Lady Malvern till the end of the week. And they expect me at home."

"Me *hopes* the lady doth protest too much? Say you would *like* to come at least."

"I would adore to, but I must get home and rescue Clarence from the lightskirts."

"I shall be in Grosvenor Square *very soon,* to rescue Prudence from her cold study."

"There is no such a thing as cold, Allan," she informed him blandly.

He arose reluctantly, pulling her to her feet, throwing his wrinkled jacket over his shoulder, and with an empty wine bottle in one hand, he pointed to the glasses. She took them both in one hand, and with their free hands tightly clasped, they strolled slowly back to the house, reconciled and happier than either of them had been for weeks.

17

The remainder of the visit passed quickly and pleasantly for Prudence, unhampered by any embarrassing questions from the other guests. Allan had left immediately without any more specific wording of a reconciliation than that he would call, but she knew in her own heart she had got him back. Maybe she was a fool to have him with his unstable streak, but when she learned the truth about the past, she could not find it in her to turn him off. He had risked his life for her. Was there a woman anywhere in the world who would not be influenced by that? He was generous too to have even spoken to her, thinking what he did. It was hard to put herself in a man's place, but she doubted she would have been so forgiving. It she had risked her life for him and he had never so much as nodded in recognition of the fact, she didn't think she would have shown him a jot of affection. That, coming on top of her novel—he must well and truly love her to want her still.

As she jogged back to London in Mr. Moore's coach, she could hardly tear her thoughts from him long enough to consider her uncle. She disliked what he was doing, disliked that Allan had a part in it, and considered means of putting an end to the studio. As it turned out, he had done it himself during the latter part of her visit to Finefields. He had put a padlock on the door and went no more to Bond Street. The cessation of his visits there was as mysterious as their commencement. He said nothing, but the golden locket was missing from his neck. His hair was cropped, and he wore a decent cravat. For the rest of it, he might as well have been in mourning. His face was miserable, his temperament not the sharp, faultfinding one Prue expected, but gentle. Uncle had *never* been gentle.

Those people visiting his studio have insulted him, she thought. He has caught them out laughing at him, and is ashamed of himself. An indirect question showed her it was no such a thing. "The lads will miss going there," he said sadly. "They liked very well to watch an artist at work. Neither Romney nor Lawrence ever had such hordes at their elbows."

Prudence thought it unlikely in the extreme these artists would have allowed such hordes in, but this was not what she said. "Why are you robbing them of their fun?" she asked in a jesting way.

"Fun? There is no longer any fun in it," he replied with a deep sigh.

"Why is that, Uncle?"

"I lost my model. My favorite model."

"There are any number of models would be happy to pose for you. Hire another."

"No, Prudence, when you have painted the best, your hand refuses to touch the next best. I have put aside my brushes. This hand will never hold a brush again."

"Who was the model?"

"No one you would know," he said, and walked away to sit in a chair by the window, gazing out onto the empty street.

It occurred to her she might discover the secret by going to the studio and studying the canvases. A positive identification might be difficult, but whatever he had put down would give an idea at least. "Have you sublet the studio?" she asked.

"No, it sits idle like myself."

"You should bring your things home, Uncle. Your pictures and canvases and so on."

"I haven't the heart for it, Prue," he said.

"Shall I do it for you?"

"That would be very nice of you. Take the carriage. I never use it these days. I don't like the high perch carriage so well as my old coach."

She was saddened to see Clarence so despondent. His painting and his high perch phaeton had been his two main joys in life. What would become of him if even these ceased to cheer him?

She went to the studio, full of curiosity, with the carriage, a footman and the key. Several finished pictures sat around the edge of the floor, for Clarence was never one to linger over a painting. There was one on the easel unfinished. It was better than the others. Not good, nor even passably acceptable, but recognizable. It was Cybele. She realized as she regarded it that there was something of Cybele in all Uncle's paintings of women. He eliminated all faults, strove for the ideal of beauty, and as he had found it in Cybele, she looked more like herself than any of his other models had. He had worked harder on it, too. There was shading in such spots as the backs of the cheeks and the temples where shading had never been shown before in his work. Yes, he had lavished his meager skill on this one till it was quite clearly recognizable as Cybele, done in the old style of Leonardo.

The girl's name, her very existence was a thorn in Prudence's side. To see her face smiling at her from the canvas filled her with the desire to take a knife and cut it to pieces. She wore a white gown and was dripping in diamonds, a slight modification to Mona Lisa, of course, that would not strike Clarence as inappropriate. Great drops hung at her ears and rested on her fingers, with a

193

slightly smaller necklace around her neck. She stared at that necklace. It wasn't possible it was the set of diamonds belonging to Clarence's late wife. No, that was smaller. Still, the setting was the same. It would be unconsciously enlarged in Uncle's painting to give it more significance. It was impossible he had given the diamonds to Cybele! This hussy had not, surely, forged her way into Clarence's life, as she had her own.

It wasn't long before Dammler's face darted into her head. *He* had got a model for Clarence. Not only the girl with the feather, but Cybele. He still saw her! She filled the footman's arms with Clarence's belongings, carrying the unfinished portrait herself. Several trips were necessary back up the stairs, but at last they had the carriage loaded and were going home.

She went to her uncle with the picture and set it on the table before him. "Is this the model who has ceased to sit for you?" she asked.

"That is she. Cybele." Clarence stared at the picture, a faraway look in his eyes.

"How did you meet her?" she asked, trying to contain the anger that fought to come flaring out. But it wasn't poor brokenhearted Clarence she was angry with, of course. He was pitiful.

"Dammler got her for me. I asked him to get me some pretty girls from his play, and he brought her along."

"I see. And why did she refuse to sit till the picture was finished?"

"She became bored with it, I think. This isn't the only portrait I did of her, Prue. There is another, better, the Birth of Venus. You will like to see it. This one I just got started, but with Dammler gone away, you know, there was nothing to amuse her in the studio, and she left me."

"He attended the sittings, *all* the sittings?"

"She only came back the once after he left. I daresay he told her not to come. He is a little jealous of me, I think. It piqued him that my atelier was such a success. A dozen times he has given a bystander a setdown when he was praising me, and he suggested more than once I oughtn't to let such a crowd in." Prudence was a little mollified to hear this. He had been trying to hint Clarence to common sense, then, but as her uncle talked on, a new fact emerged. "I daresay he thought when he told me to set up a studio that I would be a flop at it, but it was a great success."

"He told you to do it!"

"It was all his idea. He said I couldn't be bringing the actresses home to pose, and that is quite right. Couldn't do it."

"He told you to hire a studio, then brought Cybele to you to pose?" she confirmed, not wanting to make any mistakes this time.

"He didn't want me to do her, to tell the truth. He was as jealous as a sultan from the start, but she heard about me from the other girls, and in the end he let her have her way. He never can refuse her anything. He said so. Every time she wanted an ice or a sweet while she was posing, he would dash out to get it for her."

Even this she had to believe. Oh yes, when he was gone and unable to do the fetching and carrying, Uncle must do it himself. Just one little doubt lingered. She had thought Cybele must have a new patron by now. "Whose protection is Cybele living under?" she asked, fully expecting to have her ears singed for the question.

"She has been staying with old Exxon, but becomes weary of him. Dammler said he would take it amiss that I painted her, but Exxon went out of town, and he brought her along to me then. She wanted to come."

"He brought her, knowing it would alienate her patron. I begin to wonder if that isn't why he did it."

"I wouldn't be a bit surprised. That, and her begging him. He never can refuse her anything."

"Uncle," she said with a fierce eye, "the necklace Cybele wears in this painting, is it yours?"

"Yes, I talked her into it. She wanted to wear the great one Dammler gave her—earlier on, you know, before he was engaged to you—but it was so gaudy I talked her out of it. She wears it in the Birth of Venus."

This excellent folly gave her no merriment. She was too full of jealousy and fury. "Did you get it back?"

"Not yet. She wore it home, but I'll have Dammler get it for me. He will be seeing her."

"I have no doubt of that!"

"Aye, I'll take a run over to Berkeley Square when he gets back to town. I want to see where he plans to hang the 'Birth of Venus.' "

Prudence hadn't thought it was possible to find one small corner of her heart to hold any more anger; it was full of spleen, but this new outrage must take precedence. "You don't mean to tell me the picture was painted for him!"

"I had planned to give it to Cybele, but Dammler was so eager to have it, I sent it around to Berkeley Square."

"He *asked* you for it?"

"He begged for the thing. 'Name your own price,' he said. 'It would mean a great deal to me.' And a lot more in the same vein. I thought then she would pose for me again and let him have it, but once he went away, she only came back the once."

"I see. It is pretty clear what the attraction was at the studio—for both of them." She arose and strode from the room.

How had she been fool enough to trust him? How had

she let herself again be talked into thinking he was possible of reformation? He was completely dissolute. He had urged Clarence into setting up a studio and brought actresses to him, knowing her uncle was a fool. Had brought Cybele, the minute her patron's back was turned, and sat in homage at her feet while she was painted, did it to annoy Exxon so he would part with her. And then offered any price for the picture. He had always loved Cybele. He couldn't stay away from her.

She ran to her uncle's room to look around for the golden locket. She found it, tucked up in his box of treasures relating to his late wife. There it was, with the platinum curl resting in its cavity. Poor innocent Clarence had been made a fool of, lost his diamond necklace and had his heart broken because Dammler wanted his mistress back. If he had been there that minute she would have spat on him.

She had three days to let the poison fester before she saw him. She was wary. She had misjudged him once in the matter of the duel. She thought he had stayed away that time from pique, and it was possible she was misjudging him again. The picture, for instance—she couldn't believe he cherished Clarence's likeness of Cybele when he could well afford to have a proper likeness taken. But she could well believe he had asked for it to conceal it from herself. Either way, there was no decent explanation to be put on his latest exploit. At the very best it was ill-judged, and at the worst, it was infamous. For three days she watched Clarence mope around the house dismally, saw her mother worry and grow noticeably weaker, all because of Dammler. There was very little charity in her when finally he came to call.

He had got himself rigged out in his finest jacket, freshly barbered, wore a bright smile and carried a bouquet of flowers. He knew as soon as he saw Prudence that he was in trouble. She had arranged to meet him alone in the saloon.

"What's happened?" he asked.

The very question was incriminating. He knew he had left a powderkeg behind him, and had a fair idea it had exploded.

"Nothing for you to worry about, Lord Dammler, Clarence hasn't managed to steal your girl friend from you. But then I imagine you know that. You would have called on Cybele before coming to *me*."

"You found out about Cybele," he said, nerves stretching.

"Yes, I have—again. Found out all about her. But I would be interested to hear *your* version, before I jump to any hasty decisions."

"Your tone tells me you have already decided."

"I keep an open mind."

"Good. Trust me, Prudence, I can explain everything."

"Go ahead."

"Clarence wanted to paint her. He begged me to bring her around, and at last she got after me, too, and I decided to do it."

"When Exxon was out of town."

"Yes, has Exxon found out?"

"You'll have to ask Cybele that."

"I don't plan to see her."

"Are you sure you'll be satisfied with just her picture for company at Berkeley Square?"

"You may imagine why I wanted to be rid of that thing!"

"Would letting my uncle give it to the sitter not have got rid of it equally well? She seems very fond of taking things. Clarence labors under the hopes you will be able to retrieve his diamonds for him. We know *you* can refuse *her* nothing, and hope there might be some reciprocity in the arrangement."

"Oh, Lord, did the gudgeon let her get away with his diamonds? When did this happen?"

"During your absence. The gudgeon, well-named I must confess, like you, can refuse her nothing."

"Don't worry about the diamonds. I'll get them back. She's not a thief, you know. Only simpleminded. And is that the whole of it—Cybele got away with the diamonds?"

"No, Dammler, that is not even the important part in my view. The important thing is that you got Clarence to set up a studio, took actresses to him, took Cybele to him when you knew her patron would dislike it . . ."

"Now just a minute!" he said, holding up his hands. "*I* didn't *get him* to set up the studio. He did it himself. And I didn't sic Cybele on him, either. He *begged* me to take her."

"But why did you *do* it?"

"She wanted to go."

"That's no reason! You must have seen it was an abominable thing to do, and you only did it so Exxon would turn her off, and you could take up with her again yourself."

"Prudence, how can you *say* so? You *know* she doesn't mean a thing to me!"

"How can I know it? Every time I turn around you're running after her. You took her there, and danced attendance on her the whole time she was there, too."

"I only did it to hold her still so Clarence could get the damned picture done. She hops around like a monkey."

"More like a minx! From man to man, from Dammler to Exxon to Clarence to Dammler—always back to *you!*"

"All right! She likes me. I was kind to her when she was under my protection. When Danfers mistreated her she turned to me, and I gave her a bed for one night. Is that a sin? To be kind?"

"Was it kindness to help her act in a way that would lose her her latest patron?"

"She was already fed up with Exxon."

"Ready for you again."

"What happened was that Clarence wanted to paint her, and she wanted to be painted by him. I took her to the studio and stayed by while he worked, so nothing would develop between them."

"Your attention must have been all on the model. You didn't stop Clarence from imagining himself in love with her, and giving her the diamonds."

"I didn't know anything about the diamonds. That must have happened after I left. He had finished her portrait, and I thought that was the end of it. I'll get back the diamonds. That's all there is to it."

"I would appreciate it if you would do that."

"I'll do it," he said eagerly. "So, are you still mad at me?"

"Yes, to tell the truth, I am about fed up to the gills with you."

"I should have told you at Finefields."

"Why didn't you?"

"I was afraid to."

"You knew perfectly well you had behaved badly, in other words."

"Yes, I knew I had been damnably unwise."

"So you had, and so you always are."

"I don't like the sound of this."

"I don't like any of it. I don't like that she can twist you around her thumb, that you're at her beck and call."

"I'm not. It was an impulsive gesture. If I had considered all the possible consequences I probably wouldn't have done it."

"You'd stand on your head in the middle of Bond Street if she told you to."

"Don't be so foolish!"

"I don't intent to be. I can't tell you I won't marry you when you haven't asked me recently, but I will just drop the hint that any offer that spray of flowers might betoken will not be welcome."

"Prudence, you're making a mountain out of a molehill."

"No, I have been making a molehill out of the mountain of your dissolution. I don't honestly think you know right from wrong. You don't even think you have been *immoral* to get my poor innocent uncle to set himself up as a clown in that studio with the whole city laughing their heads off at him, and to trot actresses around to take his diamonds."

"I'll get the diamonds back."

"You won't get back his self respect! So far as I am concerned, you won't retrieve your own, either. You've gone beyond the pale."

"You set a pretty narrow pale," he said, his hot temper rising. "We hear a great deal about what is acceptable to the irreproachable Miss Mallow. I never thought I was auditioning for the role of Caesar's wife; only Prudence's husband. It seems the requirements are equally stringent. Not only wrongdoing but the very least *appearance* of it must be avoided."

"I don't suggest you audition for the role of anyone's husband, Dammler. It is a part that requires at least a modicum of maturity."

"On the part of *both parties*. We don't hear mentioned in this fine tirade that your only concern in the

201

matter is what people will *think*. We don't hear that Clarence—or yourself—has had the heart broken. Oh, no, you are unaware of that organ, considered vital in us mere mortals. We don't hear that Miss Mallow is a jealous, narrow-minded, unforgiving woman, always ready to believe the worst of those she claims to love."

"I no longer claim to love you."

"You did when you rang a peal over Cybele's staying with me that night. You didn't wait to hear how or why, but leapt immediately to the worst possible conclusion. The worst in *your* righteous eyes, that is. The act of love between two people seems to be considered the worst crime on your list. I consider it one of the lesser ones, one nevertheless of which I have been innocent since being engaged to you. You're not perfect, Prudence. Far from it."

"I never said I was."

"Such swift accusations as you make ought to be rooted in perfection. I think they are rooted in the misconception that you haven't a single flaw. Let me tell you, I would rather have my own dissolute character, capable of imprudent, spontaneous acts of kindness and folly, than your puritanical self-righteousness. There isn't a drop of Christian kindness in your whole body. Not *once* did it ever occur to you to inquire of me after the duel."

"I didn't know you had fought it."

"No, but you knew I was ready to, wanted to defend you. You knew I loved you, and wouldn't stay away from you for no reason. If our positions had been reversed, Prudence, I would have put my pride in my pocket and sent a note, or a word with Clarence at least. Pride is a fault too, you know, one you share with lesser mankind."

"You ought to have more pride than to carry on as you do."

"Yes, I ought. Whoever would have thought we would find a lack of any of the deadly sins in Lord Dammler? But my pride has been lacking where you are concerned. I have grovelled to you, been made a fool of in that book, been called a dog and treated like one, coming back for more with my tail between my legs. No more. I said it before and failed to keep my word. You have played Jehovah with me for the last time. I'm tired of being treated like a schoolboy who must account to his mistress for every move he makes, getting my knuckles regularly rapped for misbehavior. I'm an adult, independent human being. I make mistakes—bad ones—*terrible* ones! But I am ready to forgive them in myself, as I would be ready to in anyone else. You're not. You are unrelenting. Find yourself a fellow puritan, Prudence. You're too good for me."

"I know I am!" she answered hotly.

"Of course you know it. Your pride tells you so. But it will be cold consolation when I am gone."

"I won't need any consolation when you're gone."

"I think you will. I think somewhere underneath all those wads of misdirected religiosity there is a very nice girl, trying to get out. I see tantalizing glimpses of her at times, when her humor betrays her into humanity. We should have suited very well, Prudence. I never met any girl I liked half so well as you, but I don't intend to be measured for a new straitjacket every quarter."

"Any more insults to hurl at my head before you leave?"

"The truth hurts, does it? I didn't take it so much amiss when you used to hint me to a more proper course, but then my pride was deficient. I have no more

203

to say. I hope we aren't enemies. I don't consider you an enemy, but a misguided friend."

"It seems to me your misguided friends were always your favorites."

"You most of all, Prudence," he said, his voice pitched low, but not unsteady. There was no rancor in the speech, only regret. He looked at her for a long moment with unblinking eyes, as if he were looking at her for the last time. "I guess this is goodbye." Then he turned and left the room.

18

Clarence got back his diamonds. They came in a plain brown wrapper with a footman wearing Lord Dammler's livery. There was no note enclosed. Clarence's spirits gradually restored. He first finished Cybele's picture, then was beguiled by its beauty into making a copy, for Sir Alfred wanted one as well. He could not speak of "commissions" for a painting, which made him feel very professional and businesslike, though no money actually changed hands. Cybele became bored with the play after a while, and went back to Exxon when he dangled a rope of diamonds before her eyes. She dropped out of *Shilla* just as he wanted, and also dropped pretty well out of all minds but Clarence's. It seemed Dammler, too, had endured the break between Prudence and himself. She read in the papers that he was doing something in Parliament, had made a speech that was praised for its lucid logic, which surprised her. She had thought it would be the passionate delivery and eloquence that would be mentioned. She even met him occasionally. He had taken up Fanny Burney, and it was there that Prudence met him at tea one afternoon about ten days after the break. He was friendly, not at all angry or standoffish, as she had feared. He treated her exactly as he treated Miss Burney, as an old friend, and she was desolate. He called her Prudence, laughed and joked and argued with both of them, just as though his feelings for both were identical. She was distinguished in no small way, from the other writer in her sixties.

She still thought after the meeting that he might call one day at Grosvenor Square, but he never came. There were no scandals involving him. He was living a decent, useful life without her. It was more than she did herself. She was dully decent, but of no use to man nor beast. She couldn't believe this was to be the end of it. She was ready to forgive him again, but he didn't come for remission. After a month, she was even ready to get down to the hard chore of admitting there was some justice in his attack. She had judged too quickly, was too unforgiving. What did all his crimes amount to, in the end? He didn't lie or cheat or steal, was not avaricious, greedy, proud. He had only a hot temper, and of course a fondness for women. It was a fault of loving, at least, not hating. Who was she to sit in judgment on anyone? Hadn't she in effect lied about not having seen her book when he asked her? She had poked fun at all his friends and most of all himself in *Babe*. Even while condemning him, she had jumped at every chance to get him back, and would do it again. What a low opinion he must hold of her.

She became a perfect pattern-card of Christian forgiveness and kindness. Was never sharp with the servants or Clarence, and how she wanted to be! Really she was very hard on people. Clarence couldn't help being a fool; the servants wouldn't be servants if they were wise or clever people. Naturally one had to overlook their faults. Dammler wouldn't be Dammler if he weren't impulsive and generous and sometimes unwise. Oh, but never so unwise as herself, to have lost him! The worm of discontent gnawed away at her.

In December, Dammler patched it up with Murray and the sonnets were circulated, causing a stir around him again, but there was no outrageous behavior on his part. No private indication either that she was involved in them in any way. She heard at one of the literary do's she still attended that Dammler was "seeing" a Lady Catherine somebody or other. A girl who had lately been jilted by some fellow. That would appeal to him. An announcement, they said, was imminent. Mercifully, no announcement came.

"What is he writing these days? Does anyone know?" she asked, with just the right shade of interest to indicate that they were old friends, and nothing more.

"He has done some critical essays on drama, but he spends very little time on literature nowadays," Tom Moore told her. "They are to be run in *Blackwood's Review* starting in March."

"I look forward to reading them," she said, with only mild enthusiasm.

"They are excellent," Moore went on. "Not gay ribald tales like his *cantos*, of course. He matures in style. I must own I liked the old Dammler better. He has grown a little too staid to suit me."

"Whoever would have thought it?" she asked lightly, hiding a heavy heart.

"Usually the way with those wild young blades. They make the best men after all, when they settle down. They are more understanding from having been about the world a bit. He has certainly settled down."

"He hasn't quite settled into an old man, yet," Fanny Burney told them. "He was telling me he plans to go to Greece next spring. We may have another installment of the *Cantos* from that trip."

"Thought he was thinking of getting married?" Moore asked.

"It may be a honeymoon he plans," she replied. "Odd, the match hasn't come off yet. I know Lady Melvine is all in favor of it. No doubt she is pushing him too hard. One can only push Dammler so far, then he digs in both heels and bucks."

How well Prudence knew it!

"He's young yet," Moore answered, then the talk turned to other matters.

Prudence went home to consider that soon he would be out of the country. It would be almost a relief not to scan the streets for his form every time she went out, to go to a party without the churning in her breast in hopes of seeing him, to think every time the door knocker sounded that it was he, come to make it up at last. She was coming to realize there was to be no making up. He hadn't even been angry when he left, nor when they met since. His hot anger had turned to cold judgment against her. She couldn't believe it.

Dammler thought he had got his life under control at last. He was busy, useful, by no means dull. He attended many social functions, as many as his work in Parliament and his writing allowed. No one called him a wild buck any longer, nor was there any reason to. He had grown up. Had abandoned his lightskirts, but not women. He looked with the greatest interest at the eligible ladies, fancying himself from time to time to be falling in love with a bright eye or a flashing dimple. Lady Catherine had lovely dimples. If only he weren't so busy he might find time to fall in love with her. That there was a great gaping hole at the center of all his busyness never occurred to him. He was too busy writing speeches, models of reasoning, and essays, brilliant analyses of the works of others with nothing of himself in them but his literary judgment.

It was impossible not to entertain a passing thought of Prudence Mallow occasionally. Any mention of *Shilla* or the sonnets must bring a vision of her into mind. He wished her well. Sincerely he wished her success, and rather wished he might see a little more of her, too, for he always enjoyed talking to her. He felt he ought to explain to her why he had decided to publish the sonnets, only he didn't quite know himself, except that their suppression was given so much significance, and Murray kept after him to do it. He was always putty in the hands of his friends. He wanted to get married, so that any possible association with Prudence might become once and for all impossible. If you had to lose something you had loved, it was better to do it with a quick cut, and while they two were single, there seemed to be some invisible cord drawing him back to her. He was determined that would never happen. He *liked* her, he told himself, but love with such a woman was impossible. He could never live with her. If he patted a servant girl's head or visited a female neighbor she'd be at his throat. It was his way—he was warm, impulsive, he reasoned coldly. Still he was finding it difficult to live in London without running back to her, so he decided to go on another trip. That would give him something to look forward to, something he could really put his heart into, and till spring rolled around he would plan his route and finish getting his bill through Parliament. Writing became such a bore he hardly bothered with it. Nothing creative was possible to him.

Christmas came and went, a lonely, miserable time for Prudence; a family affair at Longbourne Abbey with his aunt and some relatives for Dammler, then it was back to London. Things became dull at Grosvenor Square for Clarence. He missed his atelier. He missed Dammler and the rest of the set that had once favored him through his niece. He could not be hard on Prudence, losing Dammler, for he knew what she was going through. His heart, too, was broken, and a foolish heart aches as hard as a clever one. He mentioned going to Bath, a stunt that had worked in the past to send Dammler running back to Prue, but she was disinterested in going. As spring hovered in the not too distant future, he mentioned a tour of the lake district, a spot he thought might appeal to her, famous as it was for a poetic colony. This, too, was spurned. It seemed she wanted to stay exactly where she was. In desperation, he hit on Cornwall—had something to do with the book she was writing, taking her an age to get on with it. Oddly enough, this bleak spot hit a responsive cord.

It sounded different enough from London and Bath to provide some interest of a picturesque nature. The cold sea, the bleak, barren rock shore and the winds appealed to her present mood. There she might get *Patience* into her proper setting, and finish up her book. That it was on the coast, and she could look at the sea carrying Dammler away from her, held the sort of morbid fascination she indulged in at that dismal time of her life. Plans were forwarded, and at the end of January they were off in the traveling carriage with four horses to go to Cornwall. She did not prevent her uncle from inserting a notice in the *Observer* to the effect they were leaving, and though it brought several callers, it did not bring Dammler. He read it, feeling a wrench inside that she was leaving, but he would be leaving himself soon, so it was best to get used to the idea of their being miles apart.

With her safely outside the city, he could think of her more often without any danger of going to her. As a member of Parliament, he could also nip into the library and scan the Cornwall papers for her name. There was no mention of her having arrived, but as February drew to a close there began to appear a series of essays of a travelogue nature about the countryside and customs under her name. He read them all eagerly, picturing her walking over the hills, thinking these thoughts she wrote, and could almost imagine he was with her. Throughout March they appeared weekly, then the last week there was none. She had left, then, would be back before he had to leave the first week of June. He would call, say goodbye to her. It was foolish to act as though they were strangers. He had never denied to himself he liked her. He would be going to say goodbye to Fanny Burney, to Tom and all his friends. Certainly he must say goodbye to Prudence Mallow and her family. He kept looking out in the London papers for her return, and began to wonder as mid-April turned into late-April and still she didn't come. A feeling of uneasiness came over him at the delay. What was taking her so long? Something must have happened.

The last week of April he stopped by Fanny Burney's to visit, thinking he might hear if she were back unannounced. He had hardly taken a seat before Fanny said, "It was too bad about Miss Mallow, was it not?"

"What about her?" he asked, while a wave of fear washed over him. What had happened? It had such a final sound to it, almost as though she were dead!

"Did you not hear of her accident?"

"What accident? I heard nothing!" His voice was loud in the small saloon.

"She was thrown from a horse in Cornwall, and was badly hurt."

"Prudence doesn't ride!"

"Does she not? Then that explains the accident—she must have been learning. I was to pay her a visit, you know. I am going to friends in Bristol and was invited to run down to Padstow to spend a week with her, but she is unable to receive me. Her mother wrote to cancel the trip."

211

"Her *mother* wrote? You mean she isn't even able to hold a pen! Fanny, how bad is it?" He was on his feet.

"Why, she didn't say it was so very serious, but she took quite a spill. Her back was damaged her mother said, and she was unable to walk."

"Oh, my God! When did it happen?"

"Early in April. I wondered she stopped writing those articles in the paper. They were very good, don't you think?"

"Fanny, you don't mean she's *crippled* for life!"

"Oh no, Mrs. Mallow didn't say so. She is having trouble walking, is all she said."

"Where is she staying? Can you give me her address?"

"Yes, but I have already written and should hear soon . . ."

"Get it for me!"

"I have it written down somewhere—Dammler, you don't mean you are *going* to her?" she asked, as she began looking around herself for the address.

"Of course I'm going."

She didn't have to ask why. His face was white, his hand trembling so she had to write the address for him. She assured him the accident was not so terrible as he imagined, but he pictured Prudence lying on a bed, racked with pain, crippled, despondent, *dying*.

While he drove at madman's pace toward her, seeing in his mind this helpless wreck of a woman, she lay on a bed of pillows, being tempted with every delicacy the county offered. Her forgiving, understanding heart and her articles had made her a great favorite in the new neighborhood. There was a mystery and a romance around her, with the broken engagement and her solitary walks over the rocks. She was thought to have done the place a very pretty favor too, to write them up in the papers. Her back did give a twinge from time to

212

time, of course. She had wrenched it rather badly when the mule—she would never have ventured on the back of a horse—slipped and she fell. She was sorry to have to put Fanny off, but the countryside offered so few diversions that if she couldn't even walk about with her, it seemed a poor idea to ask her to come. Her fall, which had necessitated her walking home alone—the mule had bolted—had been less serious than the chill she had taken. She had a bad cold, and it was really this that confined her to her bed, and made her go off a little in her looks. She had lost three pounds, which Clarence was trying to get back on her by feeding her ass's milk. The articles she had discontinued because she had already written all she could think of.

There was nothing to prevent her being up and about now but inertia, which Clarence called, and soon induced the doctor to call, melancholia, that she might have a known, discussable ailment. She hadn't the heart to get up off of her bed. For what? To face another day of walking to the seaside, of walking home and taking tea with Clarence, of saying to get away from him she thought she'd do a little writing, only to sit with a hateful white sheet before her and nothing to say? No, she lay in bed, reading novels and London newspapers a good week old that never said anything about Allan. At least they didn't say he had left, or got married. He might hear she was ill. If she got up and around, he could never hear she was ill. Oh, Dammler, you don't know the worst of me yet, she thought. You never called me conniving, but I am!

Such a long trip it was, over two hundred and fifty miles. Time to picture her not only crippled but dead, cold and buried, without ever telling her he was sorry. Why had he been such a fool? How had he imagined he could live without her? He hadn't imagined it, and he

213

knew she couldn't live without him, either. He had done it to punish her. That was it. To get the upper hand once and for all, that she not be pointing out to him how wretchedly, miserably *awful* he was. He knew she loved him; knew every time they met she hoped he would come to her. He could see her growing sorrier by the day, and wanted her to be good and sorry before he went back to her. Greece? He never intended to leave England, not alone in any case.

19

He arrived in Padstow late in the afternoon. Dusk was approaching by the time he found their cottage. When he was admitted at the door, he looked more ill than Prudence. He was haggard from the long trip, from worry, from not eating or sleeping worth a damn.

"Lord Dammler!" Mrs. Mallow exclaimed in surprise.

"How is she?" were his first words, uttered before he removed his hat or said good day.

A caller at the cottage was enough of an occasion to bring Clarence trotting into the little hallway. Such a caller as Dammler was a rare and blessed event in this dull existence. It promised a new round of social doings. If Dammler came, society would not be far behind.

"She is flat on her back," was his greeting, spoken in prefectly cheerful accents. "A terrible fall she took. She should never have tried riding, but she is so fond of those rocks out there we couldn't keep her home. She is become a regular goat for clambering over them, and writes up every trip, too. You've no idea the history attaching to that bunch of rocks. Prudence is looking into it at the library."

"Can I see her?"

"Prepare yourself for a shock," Clarence warned, while Wilma slipped upstairs to tell Prudence he was here. "She's fading away to a shadow."

Abovestairs, the mother said, "Prue, Dammler has come."

The answer was even less verbose. "Oh!" was all she could say. No more was necessary between them. It

215

was all there. Wilma could not entirely approve of him, but she was happy he came, since it brought the light back to her daughter's eyes. Got her *at last* up off her bed, flying to a mirror to brush her hair, put on a fresh cap and bed jacket. The exercise made her dizzy, bedridden as she had been for some time. She sunk weakly back on the mattress and pulled up the counterpane just as he tapped at the door.

"I'll leave you," Wilma said, feeling criminally irresponsible to do it. Her daughter didn't hear her.

Dammler stepped in, hesitant, frightened at what he would see. The crisis robbed her of color, left her limp against the pillows, her breath short. He thought she looked appallingly thin and wan, but he looked worse himself. She smiled softly, unable to keep her eyes quite dry. His impulse was to rush forward and take her into his arms, but with Clarence come upstairs and peeking over his shoulder, he could not. "So, Miss Mallow, malingering in your bed, are you?" he asked in a tone of forced heartiness. "You mean to go into a decline and become an interesting consumptive, no doubt."

"Come along, Clarence," Wilma said, and led him protesting down the hall.

Dammler advanced to the bedside. "You won't have the opportunity to lay it at *my* door, my girl."

"I don't intend to," she answered weakly.

"Society will. Who but that loose liver of a Dammler could influence a maiden so ill? Loose liver—a terrible phrase! I envisage a discrete organ floating like a meringue in custard, waiting to attach itself to something it shouldn't, or collide with an unwary intestine. I'm babbling. Forgive me." The suddenly intense expression to his last speech indicated it was not his habitual babbling he asked to be forgiven.

She smiled to hear him speak so much like himself. "Incorrigible as ever."

"No! I am eager to be corrected! I've missed your restraining hand on my grosser—metaphors. How are you, Prue?"

"They tell me I'll live. You look pale, Allan. Why don't you sit down?" She indicated a chair by the bedside. "What have you been doing with yourself? Are you doing any writing?"

"A little." This was not what he wished to discuss at all, but he took his cue from her. "Perhaps you'll look it over when you are feeling better. It will return you into the hips very likely. Hit it hard with your red pencil. It's dreadful stuff, really. Lugubrious."

"That doesn't sound like you."

He was up from the chair, bending over her. "It was me without you, Prudence," he said, gazing at her intently. "That is a different thing from me *with* you. I've missed you so," he said, smiling a smile that was close to tears. "Oh what a poor thing language is! I'm supposed to be a poet, and what do I bleat out? I miss you! A banker would do better. I have been distracted, demented, half crazy, *empty* without you. When I heard you were ill I panicked. Came galloping down at a pace Clarence would admire, with my heart in my mouth every step of the way, picturing you dead when I got here—and there's so much I want to say to you. It killed me to think I had been so foolish, so proud, so consummate an ass as to let my pride—oh yes, I've managed to corner the market on that one too!—my pride and a fear of rebuff stand in the way of making it up with you."

"No, now you are stealing my sin."

"It was worse than pride. It was vengeance. I wanted to *hurt* you, Prue, as you hurt me. And I love you better

217

than anything in the world. Here I am, spilling out my soul again, while you lie there silent as a spy. You'll have to brace yourself for one word at least. Yes or no. Can I stay?" He looked at her closely, biting her lower lip, unsure now of his reception.

"Oh Allan! Of course you can stay."

"I don't refer to Cornwall. Pray don't tell me it is a free country, as you did in Bath. Can I stay with *you*, always?"

"Yes, if you want to attach your floating meringue to this old organ, feel free."

"You have just bought yourself a most tenacious barnacle, lady," he said smiling, and reaching down he kissed the top of her head.

"Cheap at the price, too! One word."

"That, my dear heart, is but the down payment. I'll pry more words out of you shortly, when you're feeling better." He stopped and looked acutely uncomfortable, not only physically, leaning over her, but at some mental disease as well. He sat gingerly on the side of the bed. "I doubt this is approved behavior for a sickroom. Does it disturb you?"

"No," she answered, disturbed to the marrow of her bones, but in a highly felicitous way.

He grasped her two hands in his. "Prue—how sick are you? Tell me the truth—everything. I mean, even if it's something unthinkable like being bedridden for life, or a year to live . . ."

She felt foolish indeed to have to confess her malady was no more than a broken heart, that she had, in fact, been malingering, cosseting herself quite shamelessly.

"Oh, no! It's nothing like that. It's more of an—an indisposition. A sort of melancholia, the doctor calls it," she admitted.

"Fanny Burney said you had taken a spill from a horse and hurt your back."

"Oh, is that how you heard? Well to tell the truth, Allan, the fall was not serious. It was only a mule, but I took a chill, you see."

"I knew there was something wrong. I knew before I heard. I was uneasy all month. I had an apprehension something dreadful had happened to you. I should have come sooner."

"It was only a bout of melancholia."

"I've had one of those, too. You are going to be de-melancholized very swiftly, you hear? I'll come and tell you amusing stories, do tricks, stand on my head if *you* like—even on Bond Street, put on my cap and jingle my bells till there isn't *an atomy of melancholy* left in you. There's a pun for you to start getting cured with."

"The cure promises to be as bad as the disease."

"And you're too thin, too. I'll stuff you with cream and eggs and champagne and caviar to get you back on your pins in time for a June wedding. All right?"

"It sounds so agreeable I won't be in a hurry to get out of my convalescence. I might just malinger into a big, fat, cosseted, champagne-stuffed cat."

"That you won't! You'll be out of that bed and into your wedding gown we had made up last spring before June. Then you can take to your bed for as long as you like, but you'll take me with you." He laughed. "I guess I haven't changed so much after all, have I? Ever the reprobate. And I *really* thought I was cured!"

"It seems to be *me* who brings out the worst in you! You were as proper as a judge all the time you were away from me. But a cat and dog—what is to be expected of such a match but that they will fight to the finish. Nothing left but the claws and fur."

"Oh, God, Prue, I was never so miserable in my life. This past fall and winter have been an *eternity* long. The only things that stand out with any clarity in my mind are the few times I met *you*. At Fanny's remember? —where we talked about Rogers, and you said he was always building dungeons in the air? I wanted so much to follow you home that day and tell you we were doing the same, but I was too busy putting locks on all the doors of my dungeon, screwing racks and chains into the walls to torture you with. It's so good to be able to talk to you again. A bracing *soul*-ar breeze for my tired spirit. That is spelled . . ."

"Yes, I know Allan. It does not refer to the sun."

"You always understood me so completely. Words are hardly necessary between us. Yet they are our stock-in-trade with the rest of the world. I like the notion that we are different, closer *entre nous deux* than to the rest." There was a sound in the hallway, and he stopped. "I think the world is about to intrude, dammit."

Clarence tapped on the door and stepped in. "Well, well, I see you have got the roses back in her cheeks, Nevvie. There is nothing like a little bundling to put the roses in a girl's cheeks, try as we might with berries and ass's milk."

"What you required all along is a *jack*ass, you see, not a milcher," Dammler replied quizzingly, then a quick flash to Prudence, where no words were necessary to tell each what the other was thinking. There had been a prime jackass present all along.

"Eh?" Clarence asked frowning. But he was soon diverted from the riddle by more pressing interests. "I suppose you have been wondering just how soon we can get Prudence back on her legs?" he asked, and went on to answer himself. "She will be well in no time. A day or two in the garden, and a day or two to get everything ready."

"Ready for what, Uncle?" she asked with a mischievous smile, knowing well he referred to the all-important wedding that would make him uncle to a marchioness.

"Ready for anything," he answered comprehensively. He soon went on to pinpoint it a little more closely. "The dress is as good as new—the white outfit never worn and only wanting pressing. A simple note will get Lady Melvine and any other lords and ladies you'd like to have attend. You'll want a few titles for the papers."

That it would take longer than this to get a note to London was irrelevant. The nuptials were to be advanced at a speed that allowed of no more misunderstandings, even at the cost of losing a few titles. "Saturday, shall we say?" he asked eagerly.

"Uncle—it is already Tuesday!" Prudence pointed out.

"Sounds good to me," Dammler agreed, every jot as eager as the uncle.

"Well it does not sound good to *me!*" Prudence objected.

"Don't be so eager," Clarence advised in a perfectly audible aside. "You can wait till Saturday."

"You mentioned June, Allan. What of my stuffing with champagne and caviar?"

"Plenty of time for that when you are a marchioness," her uncle cautioned. "Have all the champagne you want then."

"All you can drink," Dammler promised rashly.

"More," Clarence assured her. "So, is it to be Saturday?"

The two lovers exchanged looks, questioning, hopeful.

"Saturday it is," Dammler announced, and soon found himself having his hand nearly wrenched from its wrist, while Clarence thumped his back.

221

"I'll just get a note off to Sir Alfred and Mrs. Hering and Lady Melvine," he said, and mercifully left them alone.

"Will you be well enough by Saturday, do you think?" Dammler asked her.

She felt well enough for it that very minute, and looked remarkably improved too, with her eyes glowing and her cheeks flushed.

"With a steady diet of champagne in the interval, I will be ready and waiting."

He resumed his seat beside her on the edge of the bed. "Ready for anything, as your uncle promised?" he asked with a challenging smile. "I refer—what better would you expect of Dammler—to your conjugal duties."

"Oh, yes, ready to wear my coronet. Does it have diamonds? What better would you expect of Prudence?"

"I refer, my lady, to your more physical duties."

"Ah, the housework. I doubt I will be stout enough to hold a broom for a few decades yet," she told him promptly.

"No, Lady Dammler," he leaned over till their noses nearly met, "I do not refer to the scrubbing and laundry, but the much more arduous chore of this." He touched her lips lightly. Soon he had both arms around her, kissing her hungrily, with a little sound of joy or satisfaction in his throat. Holding her close with her head cradled in the crook of his neck he said in a husky voice, "I missed you so much I wanted to die, Prudence. It was as if a part of myself, the best part, had been torn from me, leaving me wide open and bleeding." Then he laughed at himself. "I'm being gross again. You will phrase it more delicately."

"No, I won't. I felt the very same," she told him. "In fact I went you a step better and tried to die. I stopped living anyway. I might as well have been dead. You

222

were right about me, Allan, when you rattled me off in such fine style for ripping up at you. But it wasn't *just* pride. It wasn't anyone laughing at Uncle that bothered me so much as thinking I'd lose you. I was like a mother with a baby she couldn't trust, afraid to let you out of my sight, afraid I'd lose you to someone else. I wanted to *own* you."

"Now why couldn't you have told me so? How happy and proud it would have made me. And how foolish a fear it was, Prue. You can own me body and soul if you want to. You may have to wrestle Satan a little for the soul, but the body is all yours, I guarantee. The owning is reciprocal, mind. An exclusive joint company, with the two members holding on to each other for dear life. Only our paper characters will come between us from time to time. I fancy *Shilla* will want a corner of my time, the demanding wench. I'm running her and the Mogul around again in my head. A reprise you might say, as she is you, and we have had another go at it."

"Poor *Patience*. It's well I gave her the virtue to match her name. She has been as the greengrocer for three months, only to buy a cabbage."

"She's better off than *Shilla's* sheik. I left him with a sword at his neck all the way here. You may imagine what gave rise to the image. I should have marooned him in a harem, shouldn't I? He wouldn't care then if I never came back to him. But I'm sure glad I came back to you. How's that for poetry?"

"It's the most beautiful sonnet you ever wrote."

"It had the best inspiration. It's the wisest thing I ever did. Virtually the only wise thing, except for proposing to you the first time. This time around I mean to be thorough as well as wise, and get you to the altar."

"Good! I have *altar*ed my own position since last refusing you."

"Oh, Prudence, that's what I love about you! You make worse puns than I do. Now *dare* I say it? You are, you really are, my *altar* ego."

In the hallway, Mrs. Mallow heard a ripple of merry laughter, such an unusual sound in the household lately, and decided after all that Dammler would make a pretty good husband for them.